DARRYL SCRIVEN

THE DOCUMENT

A NOVEL

The Document
A Novel

v2.0

Published by Insight Fiction, An Imprint of Endeavor Publishing Group

ISBN: 978-0-9827432-0-1

PRINTED IN THE UNITED STATES OF AMERICA

For Trish

ACKNOWLEDGMENTS

In many lives, it must be admitted that someone guided us toward courses of action; even those for which we seem most naturally suited. In this way, Ernest Hill has my gratitude for encouraging me to tell stories as a way to go beyond the possibilities of academic books and reach my truest audience on multiple levels. Likewise my thanks go to Rashim Cannad & Alton Gansky, who gave helpful guidance as master technicians of the craft. Leman Raphael has my appreciation for weekly chats that encouraged this project from start to finish. Lastly, Darryl Brown deserves profound thanks for being a Philip to me; provoking me to investigate and uncover answers that I had suspected for so many years, but have now found to be much more rewarding than I ever could have imagined.

If the Gospel accounts are accurate, then we haven't been.

FACT: The Coptic Church in Egypt is one of the oldest Christian Communities and lives under constant threat of religious violence. They are almost 15% of Egypt's population, but have virtually no representation in the People's Assembly.

FACT: Apostolic Letters emanate from the Pope and have the authority of Canon Law. The last Pope to preside over a revision of Canon Law was Pope John Paul II in 1983.

FACT: There is a crypt filled with water in Egypt's Church of St. Sergius believed to have housed the Holy Family when they fled from Herod the Great.

FACT: There is an early Christian document called the *Didascalia Apostolorum* declaring that Jesus ate the Passover feast with his disciples on Tuesday evening before his crucifixion.

ONE

Rabbi Matthew Rockman ambled down the narrow passageway loosening the remaining buttons of his robe. Dampness from the rain made the cobblestone slippery, even with the gritty overlay beneath his heel-worn wingtips. His shins hurt and his knees ached. But if he had to walk over hot coals barefoot, given the last 24 hours, he'd still radiate happiness when he crossed to the other side.

If he hurried, he could get past the barricades by midnight, purchase the tickets, and be back before anyone knew he was gone. One quick conversation and he'd be on his way. A giggle escaped when he noticed the moonlight carving a path toward the landing of the ascending staircase. *It's meant to be*, he mused, sliding his fingers along the wall.

"Give me the manuscript and your death will be merciful," an unseen voice resonated.

Rockman's eyes darted, pulling in the sharp relief of an illumined silhouette blocking his path. "Who's there?"

A cloaked form emerged from the shadows like night giving birth to a demon spawn. Rockman squinted to see if the figure in front of him was real or the byproduct of prolonged sleep deprivation.

Nothing was visible, not even its eyes. The hulking mass lifted its head and stretched out its hand.

"Now."

Rockman's face glistened and his breathing labored. Only sheer willpower kept him standing. Practicing in elevators and closets allowed him to build up to the corridor, but it hadn't prepared him for this.

He dropped to one knee, then gasped and swallowed to avoid suffocation. Rockman tried to massage the hardening knot growing in his stomach, but to no avail. Caught between breaths, his neck wrenched and he couldn't help but notice how brilliantly the sky sparkled overhead. It was as if the stars got brighter the more he lost consciousness.

He'd been so careful, so deliberate. *How could this be?*

Thc crypt that gave him his highest joy would now be his tomb. The only exit stood two feet behind his worst nightmare, but it might as well have been two miles away.

"You didn't think you could escape, did you Rabbi?"

The thick, North African accent burrowed into Rockman's ears, getting closer with every syllable. As the voice drew nearer with each step, inches of the moon were blotted out and Rockman could feel his attacker's aura lurking overhead.

A Keeper! Rockman's mind blurted silent panic that pulsated from his temples down his reddening face.

Finally able to scream, he lunged forward in hopes of reaching the medieval platform. The sudden burst surprised the behemoth just enough to tip his balance backwards.

It was human after all, but barely.

With a thud, the mammoth fell onto a jagged edge while Rockman's feet clamored across his powerful torso toward the moonlight. Muffled grunts accompanied the blood trickling down the Keeper's neck.

A thin hope emerged within Rockman that he could make it until, "AAAHHHGGG!" Rockman let out a hellish shriek.

The Keeper had unsheathed a crescent-shaped dagger hidden in his cloak, plunging it overhead into the back of Rockman's thigh. The blade pierced through the femur bone and punctured to marrow. Rockman's robe prevented the blood from being visible but he could feel it saturating his pant leg underneath.

He writhed but continued to will himself up the staircase. The scrape of the frigid stone burned like dry ice against his exposed abdomen. Still, there was only one direction he could go.

Can't stop.

When he'd reached the top, Rockman summoned all his remaining strength and heaved the Medieval door ajar just enough to crawl inside.

Almost there.

Without warning, he felt a deep thud at the base of his skull. A knee came crashing down creating a tranquilizing throb. It was only seconds before the Keeper pounced on Rockman with all his weight, suffocating his prey to weaken the muscles.

"Give me the case priest. You are unworthy to know."

Rockman struggled to conceal the leather satchel, but the Keeper saw the strap protruding from beneath his shoulder. With a violent jerk, the case rose free and the Rabbi flipped onto his back.

Prostrate, Rockman locked eyes with the man whose cloak had revealed his bearded face.

"Truth will never die," Rockman hurled at his assailant.

"Perhaps not, but you will."

The last image Rockman registered was an ornate, ivory-colored handle suspended near his waist. Then, as quickly as he had come, the Keeper disappeared leaving Rockman with no more pain, no more purpose, only darkness.

TWO

Scribe was running later than usual. He'd just replaced the transmission on his Jeep Comanche and wasn't ten minutes from the mechanic before the check engine light popped on… again.

That's just great, he smirked, turning the corner on two wheels.

It was lucky for the pedestrian that she'd only taken one step off the curb. On an ordinary day, Scribe would've waited until she crossed before punching the gas. But this was no ordinary day.

Making a revving motion on the steering wheel and in his throat, Scribe took the ramp onto the freeway.

"Mandy, you've got to get me there in ten minutes or less," he said aloud.

Like Scribe, Mandy was an enigma. You could stare at her all day and still not have a clear idea of what she was. She looked like a Cherokee gone wrong. A better description was a Volkswagen Rabbit turned into a pickup truck. But Mandy had seen 308,000 miles and had never let Scribe down.

Nine minutes later, Scribe raced into the airport parking lot trying to reel in the feeling that he'd forgotten something. He didn't know if he could park in time to catch his flight to Egypt, but that wouldn't stop him from trying.

Good thing I checked-in online, he thought as he passed the sign designating long-term parking. The cutoff time to check bags was an hour before the flight. Scribe's flight left in 30 minutes.

Crossing the catwalk was painless enough and, if he could check his bag, he'd be batting a thousand.

After waiting behind two customers, Scribe placed his luggage on the scale. "Hi." Scribe handed the attendant his boarding pass and driver's license.

"Hi. One piece?" She grinned.

"Yes ma'am."

"Ma'am? Do I look that old to you?"

Trudy had just turned 50 last week and had freshly dyed her greying roots. Placing a hand on her slender hip, she tilted her head and awaited Scribe's response.

"No ma'am…uh…", Scribe checked her name tag, "…Trudy. It's just that my mama taught me to always speak to a lady with respect, no matter how young and pretty she is." He grinned back.

"You're good," she said while looking at his ID, "Mr. … Scribe?"

"Please, call me David".

"Where're you headed David?"

"Egypt. But I'm in a hurry so I need to get that bag checked fast."

Trudy clicked a few keystrokes. "Done. Is there anything else I can help you with?

"Done already?"

"Yep, and you're on your way."

"Thanks Trudy. You're good, too." She blushed.

"Trudy, I'll be back next week. Maybe I'll see you on my way out."

"We'll see." Trudy twinkled her fingers at Scribe before turning to place his bag on the conveyor belt.

This is the life, he thought. Usually Scribe flew coach, but the Administration had arranged his travel this time. The President personally asked Scribe to make the trip and it seemed she spared no expense. They'd chatted a few times at campus soirees, but he couldn't say that they actually knew each other. Besides the occasional run-ins about faculty salaries and benefits, they hardly ever spoke. Now, he'd be sure to add her to his Christmas card list.

Scribe squeezed through the security checkpoint with his shoes, belt, and laptop in hand. The overhead clock read 4:27 pm. *Three minutes*.

Bobbing and weaving, Scribe danced through the foot traffic like Mike Tyson on steroids. An elderly woman exited the conveyor belt and didn't see him in her blind spot. Scribe gently caught the matron and, in one motion, stabilized her, cut left, and continued his forward progress. Since O.J.'s image is a bit tarnished, Scribe wondered if he could apply to fill the open spot in the Hertz commercials.

This sprint through Southern International reminded Scribe of the time he broke away for an 80-yard run in High School only to be tackled at the 2-yard line. He hoped his luck would be better today.

In an instant, the echo of a crisp feminine voice across the intercom interrupted his flashback. *"Last call for Neareast Flight 441 departing for St. Louis at Gate C-29. All passengers should be on board at this time."*

Bolting toward his gate in trouser socks, the weight of his laptop became more noticeable as he cradled it past Gate C-13. *Sixteen more*.

Scribe lengthened his stride and felt the stretching heat in his hamstring. He looked down again to check that his laptop was still there.

Running through the airport was more complex than it used to be. Nowadays, you had to balance speed with control to appear non-threatening. Either that or be branded a potential terrorist. But Scribe was determined to make his flight. He chuckled when he couldn't decide if he looked more like the shoe bomber or the shoe throwing journalist sprinting with his loafers in hand.

He could see his gate to the far end of the concourse. Unfortunately, he could also see the attendant nudging the kickstand from beneath the jetway door.

"Wait!" Scribe fanned wildly with his ticket and shoes to catch her before she sealed the corridor.

Looking his way, the attendant gave a reassuring smile.

"Thanks a lot", Scribe said, slowing in front of the ticket reader, slightly winded.

"Not a problem. I knew there was one more passenger so I tried to wait as long as I could. Good thing 'cause here you are." She had a warm way about her.

First Class was no joke. Scribe had dashed for planes before, only to be told that he couldn't board because there was a 10 minute cutoff. All he could do was press his nose against the glass and watch the aircraft sit on the tarmac for another 25 minutes before heading to the runway line. That was when he flew Coach. But today was a new day.

"Since you're checked all the way through to Cairo, I just need to see your passport and you're all set."

Against the buzzing in his ears came a peculiar moment of clarity. Throwing his head back, closing his eyes, and exhaling deeply, Scribe remembered what he'd forgotten.

THREE

President Chamberlain would not be happy. She was finishing up her last round of year-end conferences with untenured faculty; the ones where she told them if they could stay or if they needed to look for a parking spot at another school.

"I get so drained around conference time, Ms. Wash", Chamberlain sighed.

"Doc, you know I understand. I've been around for 15 years and it's the same old same old."

"I'd rather fire the weak ones in mass to save time."

Ms. Wash chuckled. "Doc, you crazy."

"I'm serious. Just like that commercial. I'd line them all up against the wall and say in my best Colonel Klink accent, 'What would you like on your tombstone?'"

Bursting into laughter they wheezed in unison, "Cheese and pepperoni!"

As she recovered, Ms. Wash replied, "Doc, that sure would be funny, but you know the Faculty Union would have plenty to say about that and Human Resources would have a fit."

Chamberlain acquiesced. "Yeah, I know. But you can't blame a girl for dreaming."

It was true that Human Resources had recently stressed

confidentiality since some of the causes for reprimand or termination were considered 'delicate'. For instance there was Billy Warner, a renowned choral director rumored to suffer from the sickness of pedophilia, who couldn't keep his hands off the tenors or baritones. Then there was Mayfield Jones, a talented young jazz instructor who was accused each semester of propositioning at least three of his female students in exchange for grades.

Chamberlain would've loved to stuff pink slips into their pay envelopes and run them both out of town. The only problem was that they brought a great deal of publicity to the University. And in Higher Ed, publicity equals dollars. So she quenched her wrath by filleting the less productive junior faculty who consumed too much budget for too little return.

Between conferences, President Chamberlain sat reflecting on her last meeting with Matthew Rockman...

"Ms. Wash, you can send Dr. Rockman in when he arrives?"

"Yes, ma'am."

Dee Washington was a petite woman, soft spoken, but wise in the way that women were who had lived through more than they told. She sat in that refined way southern women learned to sit when they wore hats in church. It was a posture that said 'There's more to me than meets the eye but, right now, look at my hat'. Elegant, her hands were flawlessly manicured with clear polish on natural nails. They were the kind of hands men found themselves kissing before realizing they had done it. She was somewhere between 35 and 50, but no one knew exactly where. It was never what she said, but how she said it that made the men on campus smile like Cheshire cats.

Unknown to Chamberlain, Rockman had been in the waiting area for the last five minutes. Ms. Wash looked over in confirmation,

"President Chamberlain will see you now."

Hardly noticing her Linda Carter smile, Rockman nodded his thanks. He wiped his hands on his trousers and moved across the threshold of Chamberlain's office suite. Even though Westerville was a smaller liberal arts college, its church affiliation and academic history afforded certain luxuries to those who kept the tradition alive.

Upon entering, Rockman reacquainted himself with Chamberlain's panoramic view of the picturesque campus. The decorous office area was flanked on the left by a leather lounger and plush furnishings accented in a deep mahogany finish. Nice was an understatement. It was the kind of setting you were immediately impressed by, no matter how many times you had seen it.

"President Chamberlain."

"Dr. Rockman, please close the door and have a seat."

For Chamberlain's height, her desk seemed oversized. But she took great pleasure in folding her arms and peeking over the top at subordinates. Chamberlain motioned for Rockman to sit in one of two straight-backed chairs positioned in front. He felt that she towered above him like a monarch or, even worse, a grown-up. This, of course, was Chamberlain's intention and, judging by the expression on Rockman's face, it worked.

After Rockman closed the door, Professor Taylor entered the outer office.

"Hey Ms. Wash."

"Well, hello to you. How you been?"

"Better now."

Ms. Wash showed him just enough teeth to make him want more. "She's in there with Professor Rockman. It shouldn't be long."

"No rush. I haven't seen you in a while, but you're still looking good."

"Thank you kindly." She let a few seconds pass to marinate in his compliment. "I like that tie. Goes with your complexion."

"I figured I'd better dress to impress." Taylor leaned and whispered, "Ms. Wash, how do you stand working with her?"

"Aw, she's alright once you get to know her. It's hard being a lady in charge of a room full of men."

"True. But she ain't no lady." Ms. Wash wagged her finger and silently chided him as they shared a chuckle.

Exactly why Chamberlain decided to keep Ms. Wash was a mystery considering how she cleaned house on arrival. All loyalists to the former Administration tried to hide their allegiances and escape the guillotine. Some managed, but none of the top brass was successful. Still, Ms. Wash was not only close to the former President, but close to his family and quite open about the relationship. Even so, Chamberlain kept Ms. Wash employed. She was good at what she did and, regardless of whose side you were on, Ms. Wash knew everything about everyone who had worked at Westerville in the last 15 years. One day, Chamberlain had called her a 'Treasure of Institutional Memory'. Ms. Wash knew that meant she had the low down on Chamberlain's enemies; and that kind of person had a permanent place in Chamberlain's regime.

"Ms. Wash, it's a good thing for me she kept you around."

"Why you say?"

"Because I would've had to turn in my resignation and follow you to your next place of employment."

"Dr. Taylor, you're a mess. A sweet mess, but a mess." He looked around, feeling almost ashamed about blushing so intensely.

Ms. Wash continued. "But give her some time. It's only been two years. It takes a lot longer than that to build one relationship, let alone four hundred. She has done right by me, though. In the old days, I was considered a secretary. But since President Chamberlain took over, I'm now the Executive Assistant." She accentuated the point with a wink.

"You should be. She's hardly ever here and you practically run things when she's gone."

"I'm just saying. I've been around longer, so it's easier for me. She does get testy sometimes, but mostly my days are predictable."

Taylor shot back. "These conferences are what's predictable. I bet she's in there giving Rockman that same song and dance about increased productivity with fewer resources."

"I don't know. From what I hear Professor Rockman writes a lot, a whole lot. Doc says he writes more than anybody here."

Rockman had arrived the same year as Chamberlain and was a celebrated junior professor. His theories on the missing years of Jesus revived hackneyed discussions in mainstream academic circles and single-handedly altered the face of New Testament Studies. A young Rabbi fascinated with the story of Jesus. No wonder he and Scribe became fast friends. Not that Scribe was so interested in Jesus, but he loved to debate with the smart, Jewish priest who was.

"Oh, yeah? Well writing in science is a totally different animal. It takes longer to verify facts. Religion takes less time to write about because it's mostly opinion."

"Not for me. I'm a die hard Church of God in Christ girl. You can't join in, you got to be born in." She smiled, rocking her shoulders from side to side. "I know you don't believe in all that, but how do you think I've lasted this long?"

Taylor tilt-nodded his head on cue. "You got me on that one." Looking toward the door, he leaned back. "If he's written all that, he shouldn't need one of these meetings."

Rockman had breezed through the past two reviews and his star was rising fast in the world of biblical scholars. He was being invited all over to speak and the University was gaining visibility behind his work. If anybody was, Rockman was a definite keeper.

The meeting had lasted about five minutes. Ms. Wash barely paid attention as she filed faculty survey forms and student evaluations. These conferences were rituals at Westerville and, in her time, she'd stood by while hundreds of them had taken place.

Unexpectantly, Chamberlain's office door flung wide and Rockman bustled through the portal with clinched jaws.

Ms. Wash heard Chamberlain let out a ferocious snarl behind him, "Get the hell out of here and don't ever come back!"

With that, Chamberlain's door slammed and Rockman pulled the outer door closed without turning.

Ms. Wash and Dr. Taylor were both wide-eyed and mute.

That was almost a year ago.

FOUR

Scribe awoke but lay still for several seconds. The pulsating siren of his alarm clock beckoned him to return to this side of the universe. He had dreamed of galloping along the faces of the Great Pyramids at Giza, chasing a woman headed toward the Sphinx on foot. Just before he caught her, a wave of sound shook the scene like a snow globe. The next thing he knew, he was back in his bed resigned that it wasn't real, but relishing the receding adrenaline rush.

It was 5 am and he knew he couldn't miss this one. To make sure, Scribe had lain out his clothes the night before. The airline scaled the Cairo flight back to every two days since suicide bombs were on the rise and summer vacations to the Pyramids had taken a backseat to self preservation. Only one Neareast plane flew the route and it took two days to return. So he had already missed half of his trip. Besides that, Scribe had packed his phone in his checked luggage. Good thing he wasn't scheduled to meet the students until Friday afternoon for an early dinner. That gave him half a day to look around and form an opinion of what he saw.

Getting checked in was a breeze because he went straight to the gate. His luggage already awaited him in Cairo. At least he hoped it did. The other day Scribe felt so deflated to have forgotten his passport that he simply walked out of the airport dazed, making it all the way to his car before he remembered his luggage. By the time he returned to the ticket counter, both the plane and his luggage were gone. Boy was he glad he still had his laptop.

Scribe learned that first class passengers enjoy being rebooked at no additional charge. Due to the recent unrest in the region, he had virtually his same seat assignments all the way to Cairo.

Scribe intended to take a brief nap and transition into travel mode but, while stowing his carry-on and securing a blanket, he noticed that he was seated next to a mature and well-kept woman. Slowing his movements gave him more time to study her. Scribe had always been attracted to slightly older women, but because he spent his days on a college campus, he was rarely in close quarters with women over twenty-one.

His travel companion graciously smiled with her eyes and continued in thought. This was fine with Scribe because he wanted to gather more information about her and imagine what her life was like before he asked.

She struck him as pensive. Not in a brooding way, but like a person who took pleasure in thinking through scenarios. Her eyes, while lined, sparkled with a vibrancy that probably made all her friends happy to see her and strangers feel as if they knew her from somewhere. Her greying hair was pulled back in a ponytail and seemed to accent the diamond studs perched atop her earlobes. Her skin, an auburn tan, looked supple beneath a hemp sundress tapering at the waist and flaring to her calves.

However, the first thing Scribe had noticed was a sweet oil fragrance that lingered in the air directly above her. Now that he was seated, he wondered if it was her natural scent because he'd never smelled anything as soft and unique before; brimming with organic redolence.

After the plane leveled off, Scribe sensed a shift on the shared armrest. "I find you attractive too", she leaned and confided in him.

Scribe's head swiveled. Half-squinting in disbelief, he replayed her comment in his mind. "Excuse me?"

"I find you attractive, too" she repeated and lightly rested her hand on his forearm.

Scribe was smitten by her candor and what appeared to be an unlikely encounter with a mind reader. Had he done something suggestive, or worse, had he been thinking aloud as he often did when he was alone working out theories?

"Really?" he queried, more in awe of the moment than seeking an answer to his question.

Scribe maintained the body of an athlete. His long, lean muscles were kept taut by morning jogs, calisthenics, and Tai Chi that'd been a ritual since his undergraduate days. He thought of himself as good looking and had been told it enough to believe it was true. Still, he was amazed by the way he found himself in this conversation.

"Very", she assured. "But that's not why we're here right now." She continued, "Do you know someone named Matt or Matthew."

"Yes", he replied warily. "I know a guy named Matthew that everybody calls Matt for short. I call him Rock. He's a professor of biblical studies and a pretty cool dude. I haven't seen him in almost a year, though. We used to talk all the time."

Putting two fingers on his lips, Scribe gave her a slanted looked and changed direction. "The question is do *you* know Matt? Scribe grinned. "Did he put you up to this?"

"No", she returned calmly. "But he is trying to contact you".

"Why doesn't he just call? He has my number, email address, and more personal technology than anybody I know."

"It would be difficult for him to contact you in those ways where he is. It appears that he has been trying to contact you all day."

"Well, where is he?" Scribe raised his eyebrows.

She gently placed her other hand on Scribe's forearm, looked into his eyes and said, "He's right beside you."

FIVE

Inspector Wahid was the first responder to the emergency call from the attendant priest. As the forensic techs arrived and did their work, Wahid sat Father Timothy in a rear pew and asked him a few questions.

"Father, I'm Inspector Wahid with the Cairo Police. I understand you were the first to arrive?"

"Yes, I make the Mass in morning. Father Zizi does the noon."

"What time did you get here."

"Five a.m., everyday. Always five. Too early for me, but what can I do? I'm youngest priest and I do not have choice for this. I come through side door because better on knees."

To say that Timothy disliked waking up before dawn was far too charitable. In his mid-thirties, the portly priest had three passions: church, food, and sleep. It was difficult at times to tell for which he was most greedy. So the daily, pre-dawn rising was a prickly thorn in his flesh. But he did it because first shift fell to him as the junior priest. Not to mention, the nuns would have morning breakfast hot and ready for him after the benediction. Waking up early was bittersweet but, once he passed the bitter, the sweet was downhill from there. After doing his time as the grunt, it would be all sweet.

Wahid continued. "Tell me what you saw when you came in."

"Everything in the place, just like Father Zizi left it when he lock up after visitors." Gesturing to the right, Timothy resumed. "I come in through side door. Still dark, so I light lantern."

The lantern in Timothy's hand had lit the face of the risen Christ and made the heaviness in his groggy steps a bit lighter.

"About halfway to center aisle, I saw thing lying on floor. I creep closer and find kippah few inches away from hand outstretched." He holds his hand up for Wahid to see his robe slide down his wrist.

Swallowing, the priest replayed how he'd craned his neck to see around the front pew without moving his legs. With a gasp, he'd beheld the head from which the kippah had tumbled.

"Can you describe the position of the body, how it looked?"

"It was dark and I only have lantern light, but man wore black bekishe from neck to ankles. Like long tuxedo jacket, overcoat. Gartel around waist below something…how you say…uh... it sparkle."

Father Timothy recalled again when his feet finally convinced his fear to inch closer, he'd observed that the dead man lie prostrate on his back with his right hand extended as if it were fleeing the rest of his body. An ornate blade protruded from his abdomen, glimmering with gold flecks and surrounded by a patch of matted blood.

"After I see, I call Policia and keep doors locked until you come."

Upon Wahid's arrival, he'd had all exits sealed and made sure the parishioners were told that the Church had been burglarized. This would explain the police presence as well as buy them some time to get things figured out.

There'd been an increasing number of religious killings lately and Wahid could see that the present situation had the ingredients of a holy time bomb. Being second in command was usually an advantage. Not today.

"That'll be all, Father Timothy. If I have any more questions, I'll contact you." Wahid pulled a business card from his shirt pocket. "If you think of anything else, ask for me."

Timothy took the card and shuffled away. Wahid peered up at the crucified Jesus hanging there and said a silent prayer.

SIX

Scribe quickly swiveled his head to the aisle and then behind his seat. "Where?" He asked like he expected a camera crew to jump out any moment and yell "Gotcha!"

"To your right and a little above your head."

He turned again and saw nothing but the 'No Smoking' sign and the flight attendant call button. His jaws pursed. "What are you talking about?"

"Is your name David?"

"Yes, but how do you…?"

"David, my name is Gloria and I counsel the grieving. Dealing with so many people in the early stages of loss, I've seen many things. One is that the newly departed have a three day period to transition from us to their next stage. Until then, they hang around their bodies until accepting the separation and continuing on their journey. Some are confused and some are scared. Others are extremely lucid, trying frantically to contact people they know."

Wow, he thought. *All the seats on this plane, and I had to get seated next to a psycho.* Scribe knew they served free drinks in First Class, but this was ridiculous. He nodded, scanning her tray table for alcohol.

"I know it might sound strange, but just hear me out. After

that, I can move across the aisle to that open seat and we don't have to talk anymore. Deal?" Returning Scribe's eyebrow raise, she tilted her head to the side.

"Okay", he said in long syllables. His mom had always encouraged his curious nature, questioning everything anybody said and did. He didn't have to know the reason for a thing, but he loved to know. Scribe would ask why it always rained on Thanksgiving or why fireflies only lit up around their butts. Anything he could ask, he would. Right now, he wondered why he was sitting next to Gloria, why she was telling him about dead people, and why he had agreed to listen.

"But what does all this have to do with Rock or you knowing my name?"

Gloria considered her words while allowing time for Scribe's facial muscles to relax. "David, Matthew died recently and he's trying to communicate with you."

Scribe stared at her incredulously. Then he pulled his head back like Arnold on *Different Strokes*. At that moment, Scribe was confused and perturbed. Rock virtually disappeared into thin air and this was the first time he'd heard his name since asking around Westerville last Fall. No one had seen Rock after grades were posted and he never came back from Summer Break.

"What?", he repeated through an annoyed laugh, masking the fear that his friend could actually be dead.

"David, you must be familiar with spirits in some way or the clarity I have with you and Matthew could not occur."

She was right. He'd taught philosophy for years but nurtured a growing interest in the paranormal. He didn't really believe in any of it. Well, not that much anyway. He told himself he was just impressed with the possibility of it all. But every time he travelled,

Scribe took an entire day to hang out in used book stores, devouring texts on subjects from prophets to soul communication. The Egyptian mystery schools had always fascinated him, which is why he jumped at the chance to go when Chamberlain offered. But he'd only shared that side of himself with two people. One died three years ago and, until now, he had no doubt the other was still alive.

Raised Protestant in the southern United States, Scribe rejected the worldview of Christianity as narrow and negative in his teens. Sex and dancing were forbidden and it took him years to shake the feelings of guilt. Still, he valued the themes of redemption and sacrifice. But that didn't stop him from nursing a healthy suspicion of divine laws and people having sins. He'd pass through church from time to time, but it was more nostalgia than belief. In the first year of grad school, Scribe had gone from believer, to agnostic, to atheist, back to agnostic, and finally deciding on 'Christian Pluralist'; where he'd remained ever since.

He would always tell Rockman, "The names change but the game stays the same." They had many wee-hour talks about their unorthodox views and laughed at how odd a couple they were: a Christian who didn't obsess over Jesus and a Rabbi who did.

Still, it wasn't like Rock to go so long without a chat.

"Let's just say, for a minute, I believe you", Scribe mouthed in a detective's tone. "How did Rock die and what is he trying to tell me?"

"I don't know exactly, but I will tell you what I see."

Scribe nodded cautiously.

"Since he is communicating with you, what you hear will mean much more to you than it will to me. First, he wants me to tell you that he is alright and feels no pain."

Scribe was stone-faced, sensing his diaphragm rise and fall with each breath. All the Jonathon Edwards and Allison Dubois books he'd read helped him see that one coming. None of the dead people they supposedly channeled were ever in pain.

Gloria continued. "He wants me to tell you…'Ratboy'." She fingered her brow, double-checking the message. "Yes, he says: "Tell him 'Ratboy'."

Scribe's mouth gaped. Rockman used to call him 'Ratboy' because whenever Scribe made a good point in their debates, he would look at Rockman with his top lip scrunched close to his nose and smile like Mortimer Mouse.

"Do you understand this?"

Scribe answered or nodded; maybe both. He couldn't be sure which.

"Good." Gloria resumed. "He has an open wound to his abdomen, which means that this was a recent trauma. There are also fresh bruises on his hands and fingers."

Scribe had a quiet tension in his eyes. *Go on*, he gestured, resting a curled fist over his mouth. Rockman was the kind of guy who went around saying 'Good Morning' to everyone and always seemed to have a minute for anyone who asked for his attention. To think of him hurt like that didn't seem right.

"He is standing with outstretched arms in front of the Pyramids."

Scribe kneaded his brow and mulled over remnants of his morning dream, pulling in fragments here and there.

"Hmmh. That's weird. I had a dream about pyramids this morning." Scribe absently rubbed the stubble on his chin.

"Often our loved ones try to communicate with us in dreams. But we miss most of this because we do not know its happening."

Still off balance from the 'Ratboy' comment, Scribe pushed the crest of his lip. "What is he saying?"

He felt a little gullible; just a little. Scribe didn't totally buy the Psychic Friends routine, but he was shuffling through other possible explanations and coming up empty.

"Spirits do not communicate quite like you and I. They are on a different vibrational level. So it takes a lot of energy to make words that we can understand. Usually they can say a few things but have to show us the rest. Charades is the closest thing I can think of to describe the process."

Doubt returned. His eyes relaxed. "So he can't talk anymore?"

"Perhaps. But he is not speaking now. I feel an urgency from him, but he is only showing this image."

Scribe confirmed, "His hands are stretched out and he's standing in front of the Pyramids?"

"Yes. And he looks to be holding something in his hand; a roll or scroll of some kind."

Scribe stared over his shoulder from overhead compartment to aisle, trying hard to see what she said she saw.

He turned back. "Look. I'm not saying I don't believe you, but none of this makes any sense. I mean, outstretched arms and pyramids? I know the great Pyramids are in Cairo but, past that, nothing rings a bell."

"Didn't you say you dreamed about pyramids last night?"

"Uh-huh." Scribe nodded and flattened his lips.

"David, your dream has a definite meaning. We are taught to treat dreams as idle mind-pictures, conjured up by our day or the last television show we watched before falling asleep. But dreams are a major doorway for spirits to enter, exit, and interact with the physical plane. So the content of your dream does not surprise me.

In fact, it is clear to me that your friend was trying to contact you even then."

Scribe considered what Gloria said and accepted it for the moment. He always reserved enough skepticism to revise his opinion if he changed his mind later.

"I *am* headed to Cairo. I just figured the dream stemmed from my active thoughts about travelling to Egypt." Scribe paused, then continued. "But I don't understand why someone would want to kill Rock. He didn't have an enemy in the world."

"I'm sorry about your friend, David. In my experience, it often assists departed souls to transition if the living can resolve a problem that troubles them. Many times, this is the reason why they contact us in the early stages. They have not adjusted to their deaths yet and try to contact those they feel can help them. He must think very highly of you and your ability to understand his message. People receive messages everyday and just shrug them off as coincidence."

"Well since I don't know what Rock's message means, what should I do?"

"You will know. Even if I told you what I think, you would still have to figure it out for yourself because all the energy he is putting out is for you. So you are the only one who will fully understand the message. Just trust yourself. Stay true to who you are and focus on why you are here, now, at this moment. When the haze lifts and you see clearly, then you will know."

A few minutes later, the plane touched down and the flight attendant's voice interrupted with "Welcome to St. Louis where the local time is 8:05 am. Please stay seated and keep your seatbelts fastened until the aircraft comes to a complete stop."

Time seemed literally to have flown by as they spoke. Gloria crossed over Scribe to retrieve her carry-on and was about to deplane when he beckoned, "One last question. How did you know I was attracted to you? Did you read my mind?"

"No", Gloria replied. "Pheromones. I smelled yours and I'm sure you could smell mine. And, by the way, I'm 68."

With a flash of her eyes, she twirled and disappeared out the cabin door.

SEVEN

Chief Habash stood over the body trying to figure it out. Here was a Rabbi in full regalia stabbed to death in a Christian Church. Weird and dangerous.

"All I need are the local Jews protesting about one of their own getting murdered at the feet of Jesus."

"It does look bad sir," Inspector Wahid said.

Habash took off his cap and scratched his head. "But I can't figure out what the Rabbi is doing here in the first place? It doesn't make any sense."

"It really doesn't. Talk about role reversal."

Wahid was right. He and Habash saw murders all day, everyday. That wasn't unusual. Everything from men killing their wives to suicide bombers blowing themselves up at weddings. What was unusual was a Jewish holy man getting knifed in a church during Easter of all seasons. Not that it mattered to Habash religiously. He never showed much fervor one way or another. Habash said the obligatory Islamic prayers, got up, and continued with his day.

Yet, as a police officer in a Muslim country, the death of a Jewish Rabbi in a Christian Church during the tension of a Judeo-Christian holy week could have serious international repercussions.

"We can't have the Israeli's thinking that we're sending some kind of statement", Habash responded. "It doesn't matter where in Egypt that Rabbi was found. Jewish-Muslim relations are at an all time low and it certainly won't help things to have a murdered Rabbi on Muslim soil."

As much as Wahid hated to admit it, Habash had a point. Even if it was Egypt, the entire world had developed a way to hold Muslims everywhere responsible for things that occurred in Muslim countries anywhere. Wahid knew this well, and he also knew they had to make some major progress—and fast.

"Not that things need to be any worse Chief, but the Rabbi was stabbed with a crescent-moon dagger."

Habash grimaced. "That means Islam will take the blame if this gets out."

Wahid nodded.

"Bis m'Allah. Only God can help us through this."

Wahid paused before he responded. "God and good police work."

"Inspector, we've got a world full of angry Christians and Muslims on our hands that are edgy about a Jewish state caught in the middle. Police work can solve the murder, but it won't do much to stop people from using this to start an international revenge fest."

Wahid conceded. As he did, Lt. Saba handed him a report of the preliminary investigation and stepped away.

Giving it a quick scan, Wahid handed it to Habash while commenting. "It turns out there's not much control we have over that. The Rabbi was an American and it'll be up to the United States to determine if this becomes global news."

Habash raised his hand to cover his furrowed brow.

Wahid summarized the report. "Sir, his name is Matthew

Rockman. He's a Jewish Rabbi here under a teaching visa since last May. We found a card in his pocket for a local internet café. Do you want me to investigate?"

"Negative, Inspector. Let Lt. Saba look into it. But remind him that discretion is crucial here. No leaks about what happened until we have a suspect."

Invisibly gritting his teeth, Wahid answered, "Yes sir, Chief."

Before joining the force, Wahid read all about the great Chief Habash. He thought back to those days now and wondered what had happened.

Habash was a veteran of the Arab/Israeli wars of the 1980's. Despite his youth, he won the Egyptian Star of Valor for bravery in defending Egypt against foreign invasion. His military fame sealed the decision to appoint him as commander over Cairo's entire police force. With such an eclectic mix of citizens, the Egyptian government felt the capital city needed a leader with the perception of a domestic defender and the appearance of a young cosmopolitan.

During his first year, Habash cleaned up visible corruption in the police force. Besides the usual shakedowns of merchants for protection money, some Cairo cops were renting out their badges to settle vendettas. Investigating this, Habash oversaw two successful hostage releases and thwarted an assassination attempt by political rivals on an inexperienced and unassuming future President.

That feat earned Habash the adoration of most of Cairo's elite for two decades. It was this Habash that Wahid had joined the force to serve under and learn from. Only now Habash was serving his third decade as Police Chief, the climate of Egypt had changed considerably, and mistakes had been made.

"Need I remind you Inspector that since 9/11, training camps for Al-Qaida have popped up all over the place and Egyptian men are joining in groves? Israel's nuclear weapons have been like recruitment brochures for Bin Laden and with every suicide attack, my credibility diminishes."

Five years ago, the police corralled thousands of innocent Egyptians looking for suspects in a resort bombing. If the detainees were immigrants, it would have looked like Japanese Interment Camps in the U.S. after Pearl Harbor. When the actual culprits crossed the Suez Canal, they sent a video tape congratulating Habash on protecting nothing and jailing his own people.

Then, three years ago, a rookie fired into a crowd of voters supporting an opposition party, leaving one person dead. The press immediately called it a political murder, encouraging Habash to take the blame. And last New Year's Eve, twenty-three unarmed Sudanese migrants were 'accidentally' burned to death during a police raid, including eight small children.

At that time, the Egyptian pound had lost half its value in the last seven years with no rebound in sight. More vendors were near the Pyramids selling trinkets and twice as many children were on the streets begging. The Sudanese workers were viewed as taking jobs and food from Egyptian families. So someone decided to call in an 'anonymous' tip that the Sudanese workers were a cell of suicide bombers planning another attack similar to the resort bombing of five years prior.

Amidst mounting pressure, Habash ordered the force to drop an incendiary device on their compound to smoke them out. Instead, the device ignited the roof and the Sudanese roasted alive. Later it was uncovered that a militant cleric was responsible for the phone call but, by then, it didn't matter. The international outcry accused the police of being bought and paid for by the current government. Egypt's reputation hemorrhaged in global circles with monikers like anti-democratic, xenophobic, and sectarian hung around its neck.

This one could be messy because there was no easy way to spin it. Tomorrow's headline would read 'Rabbi murdered in Egyptian Church', and they had to find a way to get in front of it.

Wahid saw the handwriting on the wall. It was only a matter of time before the reigns of power were transferred. By right, they should be transferred to him. But that wouldn't happen immediately. So, for now, he'd have to settle for the next best thing.

"I'll get right on it sir."

EIGHT

The Keeper slowly worked his way through the dank, serpentine corridor. The labyrinth's design led intruders to a gruesome and swift demise. It would be difficult for the merely curious to find their way in, even though the entrance was never guarded and there was no door.

Humidity filled his fatigued lungs after carrying out his mission. In his mind, this task could only be performed by the most dedicated followers. There could be no indecision, no compromise.

Brooding, he relished his victory over the unevolved. *The rest aren't worthy to know. They don't even want to know.*

The passage was lit with torches burning next to each initiate's enclave. After reaching his, the Keeper set the satchel down, took off his boots, and lay on the stone floor as the shimmering rays of moonlight spoke to the ebbing tide.

NINE

Inspector Wahid approached Chief Habash who was engaging in Cairo's most popular sport: the smoking marathon. Habash seemed to try his best to smoke more cigarettes everyday than he had the day before. Part of it was stress, mostly it was habit.

"Chief, Saba found out that Rockman emailed someone named David Scribe shortly before he was killed."

"What did it say?" Habash blew a double trail of smoke through his nostrils.

"We don't know. The attendant remembered who Rockman emailed because he left without closing the screen. But after 5 minutes, the page timed out and the message could not be retrieved."

Habash plucked two specks of lint from his charcoal trousers. As a commissioned military officer, he didn't have to wear the khaki drill of the enlisted police force. And he made a point of emphasizing it.

"Oh", Wahid remembered. "He says Rockman seemed very excited about something, paid his bill, and left."

"Excited like happy or excited like worked up?"

"Excited like happy, but in such a hurry to pay his fee that he didn't wait for change."

"Interesting. So who is this David Scribe?"

"We're working on that, sir. We sent an email message telling him to contact us as soon as possible."

"Good. Meanwhile go to headquarters and find out as much as you can and how he knew the Rabbi."

"Yes sir, Chief."

As Wahid walked away, he smiled broadly, micro-bobbing his head. One thing was for sure. Habash needed him, and Habash knew that he knew. The power felt delicious. Wahid understood that Habash would be the fall guy if this Rabbi incident wasn't resolved swiftly. And after his last screw-up, the fall guy is the last guy Habash wanted to be.

TEN

March 30
It's me:

Met a beautiful woman today. Very mysterious. You all would've liked her. She told me Rock was dead and trying to contact me. I don't really know what to think. It's hard to believe but I want to. Not that he's dead, but that he tried to contact me. I feel bad for thinking this but, it gives me hope that you're still there and know what I'm saying. Did you try to contact me?

Start…Turn Off…Shut Down.

ELEVEN

Scribe deplaned at Cairo International Airport. The trip was twenty flying hours from St. Louis and it's impossible to be rested after sitting in a chair that long. Scribe felt like kissing the ground but was so disoriented from jetlag that he settled for stumbling off the plane without falling.

The scenery suggested someone dropped him off in the middle of nowhere. A jangly bus rolled up in front of the loading zone while they descended the hydraulic ladder and waited to drive them toward the front of the airport. Resigning to the process, Scribe followed the crowd and found a seat. From the window, the area looked deserted. There was a building in the distance, but the bricks were sand eroded and windswept. Scribe anticipated tumbleweeds blowing by any moment to complete the portrait, but none did.

The ride to the front of the terminal lasted a minute or two and was uneventful. Many people came to Egypt expecting epic legends re-enacted before their very eyes. The reality was that Egypt, while legendary in ancient stories, was now thoroughly part of the modern era.

Stepping off the bus, a colossal neon sign sat atop the terminal and read 'WELCOME TO EGYPT'. It seemed more like Hollywood than the fabled land of Pharaohs, but even fabled places had to ride the tourist gravy train. At least none of the bulbs were out and all the letters stood firmly attached. Noting this, the tourist in Scribe appeared.

Just as he lifted his camera, Scribe reacted to a poking pain on his shoulder.

"What are you doing?" A guard with a holstered, automatic weapon demanded.

Thinking that the raised camera explained everything, Scribe realized he was no longer in Kansas. There was a deep harshness in the guard's voice that went beyond the guttural syllables of a native Arabic speaker. Somehow the guard made the southern United States a bit more endearing in Scribe's mind.

"Shakrun, my friend. Shakrun. Thank you for helping me" *and not spilling my brains out onto the curb*, he thought. Scribe hoofed it into the airport, consciously avoiding eye contact with the guard and the down-pointed barrel of his revolver. *Some welcome to Egypt.*

Inside the terminal, bags lay on the opposite side of the security checkpoint. The guy at the passport window was obese, early forties, with a glaze of caramel tinting his teeth. He slouched a bit as he inspected each set of travel documents, like he could have you carted off to jail with one grunt to his compatriots.

Scribe stepped forward, deciding against small talk, and handed over his passport. The guard held out his hand again and gave Scribe an apathetic once-over. The quizzical expression from Scribe triggered Yuck-Mouth to roll his eyes.

"Visa."

"What visa? Nobody told me I needed one."

Scribe could feel the stare of the first guard burn a hole into his back. The passport sentry straightened and a hand came through the Plexiglas opening. "Fifty."

"Dollars?", Scribe gasped.

"Egyptian Pounds", the man returned.

"I don't have Egyptian Pounds. I only have ten dollars and a credit card." Scribe produced his wallet to prove his statement.

"Looks like you have wrong visa", the guard scoffed, causing a tingle to form on the nape of Scribe's neck.

Yucky popped his knuckles and thrust a short, chubby finger toward the door.

Fighting the urge to look back, Scribe remembered the greeter he met on the way in. Big, six foot four, burley, clean shaven. The dude looked like he could smile at you while rendering you unconscious; the kind of guy you'd expect to hurt you just for exercise.

This was crazy. Who ever heard of getting kicked out of a country for not having cash? In that moment, Scribe empathized with immigrants in a way he never had. All the stories he knew suggested people had trouble leaving Egypt, but never trying to get in.

On reflex Scribe jumped. Two meaty hands had grabbed his shoulders. Spinning free, he found himself glaring into the jaw line of the greeter. The gun was still holstered, but the greeter's scowl smacked of insult. Scribe clenched his fist preparing for the worst.

The other people in line hoo-shooed about Scribe's plight, but nobody stepped up to help a fellow American. It may have been wishful thinking, but he felt intensely offended that his countrymen would stand there voiceless while he squared off with Andre the Giant. Coupled with umbrage, a brief pang of disbelief flitted across his mind as the vacationing onlookers attentively permitted him to meet his doom. At least there would be witnesses to tell the American Embassy how he died.

Instead of pouncing, the greeter gestured dismissively and

Scribe leaned around Goliath to see a sign in English near the airport entrance:

MONEY CHANGER: CASH, CREDIT CARDS, OR TRAVELLER'S CHECKS ACCEPTED

The laughter of the two guards angered Scribe more than their little joke.

Finally through the checkpoint, bags were strewn all over the floor. Half scrambling, half wandering, passengers went to and fro retrieving their belongings. Scribe figured his bag wouldn't be there so he looked around for an employee to direct him to the lost luggage counter.

As he did, he saw guards with machine guns strategically stationed around the area in green fatigues and boots. *Here we go again*, he thought while scanning the vast expanse. Taking off his shoes and belt in U.S. airports didn't seem as intrusive as it had yesterday.

From the corner of his eye, Scribe spotted a handwritten sign with a familiar word. Turning, he realized the word was his name and the person holding it had his duffle bag at her feet.

She was around 5'8", had brownish-red hair that hung 2 inches past her shoulders, and eyes that seemed to change color as he moved closer. They were either greenish grey or grayish blue. But whatever color her eyes were, they were piercing and strong, alluring. She had an olive complexion deeply tanned by the Egyptian sun. Layered, a button down cotton shirt hung open with the sleeves rolled up. Underneath was a fitted, azure-blue tank that displayed an impressive core and well-framed top. Her skirt was long and flowed to her ankles, lightly draping her shapely hips.

It was traditional, but her style gave the look a special savoir faire. Oddly, she wore a pair of running shoes that were fashionable, but didn't accentuate her ensemble. It didn't matter. To Scribe, she was an oasis in the desert. Her expression was intelligent and sultry; a welcome feminine sight in a sea of machismo and machine guns.

She peered at Scribe, knowing he was the man she waited on. He wondered if the lady with the sign could smell his pheromones flying toward her.

"Dr. Scribe?", the sign bearer asked.

"Yes".

"My name is Mari and I will be your guide during your stay in Cairo."

Mari spoke with the accent of a native Arabic speaker who'd learned English at an early age. Since it was her business to guide tourists around Cairo, languages were one of her specialties. She'd mastered seven so far and was working on Swahili in her spare time. All those clicks made the language a little more difficult.

Tourists from Europe and the United States had the strongest currency, so she made sure that English, French, Spanish, and German were at the top of her list. Mandarin Chinese and Portuguese rounded out the bottom.

Scribe noted her firm grip. "Nice to meet you, Mari. I see you found my bag."

"Yes, the University tag is still there. It arrived two days ago and I retrieved it from the luggage counter this morning."

"Thanks. Uh Mari, tell me something. How did you know I was me?"

"Your President, Dr. Chamberlain. She informed me that you missed your flight and that you would be arriving today. She described you as an American, tall and handsome, relatively, with dark brown eyes carrying a laptop."

How did Chamberlain know I missed my flight? Well, so much for her not finding out.

"Did she say relatively tall or relatively handsome?" Scribe was fishing. Not that he cared what Chamberlain thought of him.

Mari smiled courteously. "Right this way, sir."

TWELVE

Chamberlain returned to her office after the annual luncheon with the Board of Supervisors. She'd received confirmation that her contract would be renewed if she could steer the University clear of any public scandals. A recent scare involved two faculty members fighting in the chemistry lab about plagiarism and stolen data. It had gotten violent.

Dr. Burke threw some graduated cylinders at Dr. Lin, which got the AAUP and local police involved, bringing a lot of bad press. Chamberlain managed to quash the situation by getting the scientists to share the research and accept equal credit. The Board had been pleased with her resourcefulness, rewarding her with a vote of confidence and a raise. However, all of this was contingent upon her keeping things under control until the next fiscal year began.

Aside from the occasional amorous relationships that went sour between administrators, her Vice-Presidents handled the faculty and student issues. Her staff pretty much had Warner and Jones cornered with the threat that their retirement benefits would be forfeited if the authorities ever had to intervene in their little 'after school sessions'. However, when it came to matters where students represented the University or donors were concerned, Chamberlain handled those matters personally.

When Chamberlain walked into the outer office, Ms. Wash was typing invitations for the Unity Celebration.

"How was the meeting?" she asked.

"Fine."

"Did you bring me something from lunch?"

"Sorry, Ms. Wash. I forgot. I was so focused on the meeting that I didn't even pay attention to the food. You know we girls have to play hard in the boardroom. Letting your hair down is considered a sign of weakness."

"But men do it all the time."

"You're right. But double standards aren't about fairness. They're about power. And if you want power, you have to put up with them. By the way, did you email Dr. Scribe about the incident?"

"Yes, ma'am. I did it yesterday but he hasn't responded yet. It's not like him to delay a reply. He's usually online day and night."

"I know. But he had a little setback. He missed his flight and failed to alert us. Yesterday afternoon, the travel agency emailed to confirm his new itinerary. I waited to see if he would call, and he didn't. Typical. Men have problems acknowledging women as authority figures and try to get around it any way they can. That's okay, though. It's hard to get around us when we pay the bills."

"You're right about that, Doc. But Doc, Professor Scribe is a nice man. He's charming and kinda cute."

"Uh-huh", it's the cute ones you have to watch. Let me know when he replies. I need to make sure this Cocoa thing doesn't get out of hand."

THIRTEEN

Mari led Scribe through customs and the double exit doors. It was like the sea of skycaps and drivers parted as they walked through. Each turned to her and gave a conciliatory wave. You would've thought she was the Queen of Sheba and that they were trying to stay in her good graces. As she passed the soldiers wriggled their fingers and, to their delight, she called each of them by name.

Given his earlier bout with the dynamic duo, Scribe was impressed by how freely Mari moved around the airport. She had access to parts reserved for employees only and appeared unphased by the heavy artillery carried by the welcoming committee.

"Hey, you know these guys with the machine guns?"

"Yes. In a sense you can say we work together."

"How's that?"

"We have an agreement. They let me get my customers' bags and greet them at the gate, and I don't give them a hard time. More tips for me, more tips for them."

"Right", Scribe drawled.

"Indeed, they keep the tourists safe on arrival and I keep them safe when they're in Cairo. We all need tourists to live and so we work together."

Jolting his head back slightly, Scribe responded, "Humh. I've been on a lot of tours, but I've never had a guide be so candid about our relationship."

Mari stopped pushing the cart. "Does that offend you, Dr. Scribe? My candor?"

"No, not at all. No need to apologize."

"Good. Because I wasn't going to. I'm just trying to understand what kind of man I'll be spending the next three days with."

"Oh", Scribe nodded like a washed up gigolo.

Recovering, he inquired, "Well, what do you think so far?" He knew it was risky and could flush their chemistry down the toilet if it backfired. But it was an emergency maneuver.

"I'm still thinking", she sniped before flashing a playful twinkle in those grey-green eyes.

The response lifted Scribe's confidence. Still, he didn't quite know how to read Mari. Not yet. But he did know a smile from a woman was always a good sign.

When they'd reached the curb, Mari unlocked a midsized vehicle that looked like a cross between a Volkswagen Bug and a commercial passenger van hit by a shrinking ray. This was the true meaning of a *hybrid* car. Scribe fought off getting down on one knee to propose.

"Interesting car", he said, eyes taking in every inch of the odd automobile's features.

"Yes, this is my Vinta. It's my livelihood. 500,000 miles and still runs like an Arabian horse."

"Well, that's quite a shelf-life."

"What is this 'shelf-life'?", she asked.

"It means", he searched for the words to explain. Finding them, he said, "It means it's lasted a long time."

"Yes. I understand. It has." Scribe reached into his luggage and retrieved his phone before Mari closed the hatch. Mari switched gears. "We should go. You have to get checked into your hotel. I'm sure you are tired from your journey."

"I am. A bath and a change of clothes would be great."

Scribe had traveled most of North Africa, but never to Egypt. People in Morocco and Tunisia had hard lives. And not much could grow in the arid temperatures of Israel. Constant heat was enough to make anybody irritable.

Yet, despite the welcome brigade, Scribe noted a lightheartedness about the Egyptians beyond baggage claim. Cabbies were hustling fares and offering to guide tours 'anywhere you want to go'. Like it or not, it was a living. Early mornings and late nights were a staple for working class folks in most of the world. But instead of complaining about long days, the Egyptians he saw took time to have tea on the hoods of cars, laugh, and many male friends held hands as they walked down the street. Maybe the Pyramids and Sphinx put smiles on their faces, or maybe it was something that tourists couldn't see or bargain for.

At the stoplight, Mari removed her top shirt and tossed it onto the second seat. Scribe slanted his eyeballs. Squirming, she slid her skirt down over her feet and handed it to Scribe.

"Would you fold that and put it on the seat behind you please?"

"Sure", Scribe said discomposed. As he folded the skirt, Scribe glanced over, inspecting the muscle line running along the curvature of Mari's seat. She was soft, but strong. Not too thin; definitely built for comfort. Scribe did his best to focus while he turned to lay the skirt on the backseat. Now her running shoes made sense with her outfit.

"Thank you Dr. Scribe. I am much more comfortable."

Me too, Scribe thought.

"I wear the skirt and top in the enclosed areas. It is custom but also a business precaution. Are you at ease with my attire?"

Scribe looked her over with the heart of a frat boy. "I'm cool", he replied shrugging his shoulders.

He hoped he'd pulled back enough from his initial reaction but wasn't sure Mari bought it.

"Dr. Scribe, your President said that you should check your email when you arrive. There's an internet connection in your room if you wish to check it there."

"Thanks." *I wonder what she could want. Probably chew me out for missing my flight.*

"I don't know the issue, but she sounded urgent."

"I'll be sure to let her know I made it."

It took about fifteen minutes to drive to the hotel. The streets were crowded and drivers honked their horns endlessly. Scribe thought Manhattan was the worst, but he'd changed his mind since leaving the Cairo airport. None of the cars had recognizable names. The only requirements seemed to be that they worked and could endure multiple wrecks.

In Cairo, the cars were big enough for passengers and small enough for go-cart traffic. Scribe saw a three hundred pound guy crammed into a compact car looking like a child trapped inside a covered Big Wheel. There must be an Egyptian law against mufflers because the exhaust fumes were so strong, the smog made Scribe cough even with the windows rolled up. If the police ever wanted to gang up on somebody, they should hit the guys stealing all the mufflers.

Squeezing between them and the compact, a small Asian import whizzed by, barely managing not to shuck the mirror off Scribe's side of the vehicle.

"Whoa! Did you see that fool?" He jumped close to Mari staring.

The expression on Mari's face told him she hadn't batted an eye and couldn't be less concerned about the level of recklessness engulfing them.

Looking straight ahead Mari's only words of consolation were, "Welcome to Cairo."

The guy in the import slowed to sandwich between two trucks with plywood rails above their beds forming makeshift goat pens. Nobody seemed to care that Mr. Bumper Car scraped the side of the trucks as he passed, least of all him.

When they pulled up to the hotel, Scribe felt like he'd made it through the signature ride from Theme Park Hell.

Mari offered him a napkin. "Are you fine? Your pupils are smaller than they were a few minutes ago, yet your forehead is still moist."

"I'm fine. Nothing a little fresh air and a hot bath won't cure." In the corner of his eye, Scribe spotted a white paper bag on the back seat rolled the way that people wrap food. "What's in the bag?"

"Shawarmas."

"What's that?"

"It is similar to a gyro with chicken or lamb, purple onions, lettuce, sauce, and other toppings."

In all the excitement, the aroma of Scribe's fear must've blanketed the smell of the food. Now that he was safe, his nose was working again.

He went into game mode. "Mari, I know we just met and that food is personal, but do you think I could have one of those…sha-war-mas"? He stumbled over the word intentionally. "I'm starving" he added, nailing his best impression of a lost puppy.

"Yes, I can spare one." She harrumphed graciously. "I will park the car and meet you in the lobby in one hour. I have phone calls I need to make. Meanwhile, you can get settled and enjoy your first Egyptian meal."

FOURTEEN

When Scribe entered the Semiramis Intercontinental Hotel, he wasn't prepared for that level of splendor. The lobby featured ice-sculptured swans and tropical foliage accenting the foyer. On his left were two, open-air cafés whose ambiance came from the waterfall serving as their backdrop. Walking further, Scribe passed a five-star restaurant boasting a constellation of Egyptian symbols overhead. At night, the center stairwell lit into a dazzling display, making guests feel that besides a trip to the Great Pyramids, they could easily stay in the hotel the rest of their visit and not miss a thing.

The front desk staff treated Scribe like royalty. Chamberlain had already paid the tab and put some extra money on his account for meals and incidentals. So when the porter lingered after bringing up the bags, Scribe felt the least he could do was give a good tip.

The suite was exquisite, in the heart of downtown Cairo. Plush crimson carpeted the cavernous space leading to drapes tasseled with gold and silver strands. In between stood a princely footboard carved from the finest cypress in Egypt. The spread showcased an array of diamond patterns embroidered in a raised style of such craftsmanship that Scribe wondered if it was acceptable to touch or sit on it. A handsome cherry oak desk rounded out the main furnishings with a high back chair and instructions for accessing the internet nestled in front of the guest services manual.

Scribe parted the thick drapes and allowed natural light to flood the room. The luxury of the suite prepared him for the majestic view that had to accompany placement on the 29th floor. Painfully, Scribe saw the disappointment on his face in the window's reflection.

Instead of Pyramids, he found himself looking at the tops of dirty high rises, abandoned buildings, and dilapidated billboards advertising cigarettes and alcohol. All of this, right next to the fabled Nile River with a hazy cloud of smog and armed sentry patrolling the streets.

Closing the gossamer curtain underneath the drapes, Scribe sighed and headed for the bathroom to wash off the chagrin. Upon entering, the magnificence of the wall etchings seized him immediately. It was as if all the pageantry of ancient Egypt and its palatial mythology converged in the lavatory to inspire, awe, and restore.

He took a shower, noting the cream marble covering the floors and counters. Everything was gold-plated: the faucet, the towel rack, even the toilet. But, by far, the most stunning feature was the gold-plated telephone mounted by the toilet. "Easy access", he thought aloud.

Then, something odd occurred to him. Scribe realized that his bathroom had two, slightly different, toilets. One was normal while the other had what looked to be a golden doorstopper leaning down into the commode. No seat, no lid, just the doorstopper. Scribe lifted it and water shot into his face. He lowered the doorstopper and decided he'd use the toilet that looked most familiar, just to be safe.

Feeling clean and refreshed, Scribe put on the terrycloth robe hanging from the door and went out to explore his meal. Maybe it was because he hadn't eaten in twenty one hours, but he believed that shawarma was the best thing he'd ever tasted. He savored every bite and almost forgot he was on a time schedule. With the last chomp, all he could do was wonder if Mari had eaten the other one.

Scribe had about fifteen minutes before he was to meet Mari in the lobby. He spotted the T1 connection by the telephone jack and was online in an instant. Beyond his usual correspondence, he had two messages that stood out: one from Ms. Wash for President Chamberlain and the other from an Inspector Wahid. The text of Ms. Wash's email read:

> April 12th
>
> Dr. Scribe:
>
> President Chamberlain asked that I contact you to handle an unpleasant situation. One of our exchange students, Cocoa Santana, was involved in an altercation with another woman in her work-study office. You know Cocoa can be quite expressive and, apparently, she was arguing with the woman about politics. However, Cocoa has been causing quite a stir since the incident; so much so that the director of the program in Egypt has considered canceling the student exchange due to irreconcilable cultural differences. We need you to try to bring some balance to the situation before the Choir performs at the Unity Concert on Saturday evening. Lots of dignitaries will be there and it's vital to the program that this is resolved amicably. Please try to calm Cocoa down and explain to her

what's at stake. Reply to acknowledge you have received this message.

Sincerely,

Dee Washington for President Chamberlain

Oh great. I have to stave off an international incident in a foreign country over the weekend. That's swell. I'll ask if they need me to find Bin Laden while I'm at it...Reply...Send...Next message...

April 12th

Greetings:

This message is for Mr. David Scribe. Mr. Scribe, a serious circumstance has occurred involving Matthew Rockman at St. George's Church. We retrieved your email address from a computer terminal he used, but we do not know the content of the message he sent. We need you to contact us as soon as possible and would appreciate you forwarding Rabbi Rockman's email message to us. If by chance you are in Cairo, please come to our downtown headquarters and ask for me. With reasons of diplomacy, discretion is essential in this matter. My contact information is below:

Inspector Lamir Wahid

Cairo Police

145 Al Kosheh

cairopolice@egypt.net

Scribe stared at the screen in a daze. He was speechless, even though he knew somehow that Rockman was dead the first time he heard it. As the conversation with Gloria flashed before his eyes, pain began rushing to his mind like a flood of bad childhood memories. *What happened? What was Rock doing in Cairo?*

In all the confusion, Scribe had never taken time to grieve for his friend. He only half believed it then, but now the attempt of the police to conceal what happened told him everything. Besides that, he hadn't had the personal space to grieve. He still didn't. Trying to summon his thoughts from the edge, the avalanche hit without warning. All he could do was bury his face in the elaborate bedspread and weep.

FIFTEEN

Inspector Wahid rested an index finger on his lips and pondered possible motives for Rockman's murder. He knew that Habash wanted something that he could tell the politicians, for no other reason than to keep them off his back. For years Habash had been under threat of replacement due to the public outcry against police brutality. The higher ups had managed to avoid responsibility for their mistakes, mainly because Habash was always so willing to shoulder it instead. That 'hari-kari' trait was part of his constitution as a soldier but, as a political appointee, it made Habash a convenient scapegoat when the people wanted a governmental sacrifice.

There was also a rumor circulating around the department that Wahid constantly positioned himself to become the next Chief by trying to solve cases in a way that ensured he got most of the credit. The possibility that the rumor was true didn't sit well with Habash. Habash wasn't sure, but there were a few cases that he got chewed over while Wahid made the newspapers. Even if the rumors were true, Wahid hadn't solved enough recent cases to make a move like that; which left Wahid vocationally vulnerable. So he either had to gain traction on this one fast or Habash would hammer him out of sheer panic.

"Here's what I found, sir." Lt. Saba handed Wahid a printout with a color photo in the right-hand corner.

"Huh...philosophy of religion, conferences in Wales, Capetown, and a Fulbright? This guy covers a lot of ground. I wonder what he has to do with all of this?

Saba continued. "Taught at the same American school as Rockman, uh...Westerville University. It's a Catholic school."

"Anything else?"

"Yes. About three years ago, his wife and daughter were killed in a car accident. Drunk driver trying to elude capture went up the wrong ramp on the Interstate Highway. Head-on collision killed them instantly. They were less than a mile from home."

"This guy's had it rough. We both know sorrow comes in bunches." Wahid leaned back in his chair. "I'm not looking forward to telling him his buddy got murdered."

"Inspector, something else that might interest you is that Scribe was confirmed on a flight to Cairo two days ago. He should already be here."

Wahid inhaled, held it, then exhaled. "So Scribe shows up on Wednesday and we find the Rabbi murdered on Thursday. Pretty coincidental."

"Yeah. Seems his school is part of the Student-Exchange Program and their musical group is singing at the Unity Concert tomorrow evening."

Wahid mumbled something in Arabic. "I'm trying to keep this low key and the city is bringing attention to the whole thing. Since when do Muslims party with infidels?"

Saba grinned uncomfortably.

Sensing this, Wahid shifted away from the silence. "So what's the scoop on Rockman?"

Saba paused in passive protest, but remembered he'd been addressed by a superior officer. "He taught Christian religion, specializing in the New Testament. He has many cited articles on the historical Jesus and the chronology of the biblical Gospels."

Wahid's mustache lifted. "They really mix it up in America, don't they? Rabbis studying Jesus at Catholic schools? Next they'll be studying Hitler."

Saba didn't bite at Wahid's attempted humor.

Wahid tried a different tact. "Let's say Scribe murdered the Rabbi. Do we have motive?"

"Nope. Besides working together, I don't see anything suspicious."

"Me either. But it would be better for all of us if an American killed the Rabbi."

"Now that I agree with." Saba gave him a scolding smile.

Wahid held up both his hands. "Okay, okay. I'll lay off the Islam party jokes. Don't be so sensitive."

Wahid and Saba had come into the precinct and worked on many homicides together. Two years ago, Wahid got promoted and Saba found himself working under his peer. A lot of the guys in the Department poked fun at Wahid before he made Inspector. Wahid thought he was entitled to a little payback.

"That's all I have now, sir."

"That's plenty. Thanks Saba"

Saba shrugged. "We still haven't heard from him. When we do, I'll let you know."

"Right."

Wahid picked up the paper and stared at Scribe's passport photo. *Why are you here and how can I place you with the Rabbi?*

SIXTEEN

Scribe wiped his eyes and exhaled audibly. Besides dealing with the death of his friend, he was also expected to avoid a public relations crisis for the University *and* help in Rockman's murder investigation. Kind of insensitive, but nothing he could do about it. By nature, he was suspicious of the police. But if they were trying to help... Just then he had a thought.

What email? There was no message from Rockman in his new mail folder and Scribe was sure he hadn't opened any messages since his plane left the States. Scribe checked his spam.

Scanning the bulk mail felt like wading through rejection letters. It was ordinarily a pointless exercise but, every now and then, he found a stray message sent by someone he actually knew. It was rare but worth a shot. Opening to the last page of bulk messages, Scribe froze. *There it is.*

He hesitated before clicking on the message line which simply read:

<u>I Found It!</u>

Click...:

April 11th,

Dear Dave,

I'm in Cairo. It took me almost a year, but I finally found it. I don't have time to go into it now, but I promised to tell you the moment I found out. I can't wait to talk. I've attached the key to it all as a Word document. Man, it'll be good to see you. Sorry it took so long to let you know where I was. Just know that I would've if I could've. I'll explain it all later. Gotta go, phone is beeping.

Matt

You found it? You found what? Scribe tried to decipher what in the world Rockman was referring to.

Their conversations were so full, Scribe didn't know where to start. He and Rockman talked of gods and possible worlds, politics and economics. Anything they could fill a night hashing out, they did. Though, without question, their favorite topic was the Bible.

They'd spar deep into the night and clashed constantly on ways to explain biblical discrepancies. One would ask the question and the other would try to give a plausible answer. Then the questioner would shoot holes in the answer and offer another. For instance, Scribe might say:

"Okay. How do you explain Cain's wife if there were no other people on earth besides Adam, Eve, and Able?"

Rockman would reply, "Easy. She was his sister. The guys that wrote Genesis didn't want to detract from the murder story by telling us Cain and Able had a sister. What's more interesting: women or murder? Don't answer that." Then he'd laugh.

Rockman was funny like that. He could give a critique of ancient chauvinism, but not come off preachy. He was a self-professed, male feminist who harped on the misuse of women in the Bible to tell men's stories.

"They just didn't want to tell us about her because she was probably the firstborn and outranked her brothers." Rockman would then yield for any rebuttals.

Scribe would follow, "Right. But what about the other dudes Cain is scared will kill him if they find him? Where did they come from? These aren't women so you can't blame sexism on them being downplayed, too. It looks to me like people are just popping up all over the place whenever the author needs some more characters."

Rockman would comeback, "Dave, you know sibling rivalry plays better than a group of guys standing around scratching themselves. For all we know, Cain and Able could've been fighting over their sister while their other brothers were gathering figs." These answers wouldn't satisfy Scribe, but amused him because they were thoughtful and lighthearted.

Not that much was at stake for either of them in the discussions. Alongside Scribe's Christian Pluralism sat Rockman's Jewish Atheism. The fact that he was a Rabbi was cultural and had more to do with his appreciation for the idea of God in people's lives rather than his belief in an actual God. He was born a Levite but only decided to be active in the priesthood after seminary. A few priests had suspicions about his theological views because they rarely heard him debate publicly. But, because of his family lineage, cultural association, gentle disposition, and vast knowledge of Jewish religious texts, no one ever asked him what he personally believed.

And he was never tempted to volunteer any direct hints, except with Scribe. They would talk all night about the comparison between Greek mythology and Jewish mythology, Eve and Pandora, Hercules and Sampson, Dionysus and Jesus. But their favorite topic was Jesus. Always Jesus. They would go back and forth about whether there was a real, historical Jesus or if he was a character, like Socrates, created to represent, in Jewish terms, the ancient wisdom that periodically surfaces to help humanity along.

Rockman argued that Jesus was an actual person that was really crucified but wasn't God. Scribe thought that Jesus was not a person at all, but a consciousness that gained momentum through texts and followers who were ready to embrace the next level of human development. They both gave compelling arguments, but neither had more conclusive proof than piecemeal theories. They'd agreed about a year before Rockman vanished that if either of them ever found proof, the other would be the first to know.

Could it be? Scribe wondered while he considered the attachment icon. The possibility was too much to fathom. As he opened the document, what appeared were fragments of texts that seemed to be Greek. Scribe recognized common words from his undergraduate days but had moved toward French in graduate school. He needed help and knew just the guy for the job. But first he had to get downstairs to Mari and sort out how he was going to deal with the Cairo Police, Cocoa, and figure out if these fragments could tell him what Rockman was intending to.

SEVENTEEN

Scribe exited the elevator to see Mari settled in a loveseat next to the currency exchange. She tapped the keypad of her telephone as he approached.

"Hey, Mari. Sorry I took so long."

"Not a problem. I used the time to return calls and respond to some email. Are you ready?"

"Yes."

"What would you like to see first? The city or the Pyramids and Sphinx?"

"Nothing just yet. Some things came up and I need to figure out how to handle them and in which order."

She noticed that he didn't have the gleam in his eyes from before. His rims and tear ducts were still puffy. "What has happened?"

Scribe lowered then resumed his gaze. "For starters, I think my friend was killed here in Cairo and I don't know why. Then the police sent me an email requesting my 'cooperation' in their investigation."

"Oh, no. I'm so sorry to hear about your friend." She moved closer and searched his expression. "But how can you help the police?"

"Well, the cop that contacted me wanted to know about an

email Rock sent me. I guess Rock sent it near the time of his death."

"I see." She paused respectfully. "How did it happen?"

"They didn't say. All I know is that a local church was involved."

"What church?"

"I think St. George's. It's probably Catholic."

"Actually it's Greek Orthodox, before that it was Coptic. For centuries the ownership alternated between the Copts and the Greeks. However, since the 1400's it has remained Greek Orthodox. Still large numbers of Copts and even Muslims visit on Fridays and Sundays. It's about 5 kilometers from here. I always make a stop there on my tours."

"I wonder what Rock was doing in a church? He didn't think much of organized Christianity. He'd always say he and Nietzsche loved Jesus but couldn't stomach the Church. If he told a true believer something like that, things could've gotten violent."

"I do not know, Dr. Scribe. But it can be very dangerous in Old Cairo, especially after dark. The poverty and religious tension make crime inevitable. Because of tourists, the area is usually policed. If the police need your help the attack probably happened at night, after the patrol passed through that section." Mari's sudden shift from compassionate to deductive both alarmed and aroused Scribe. After a few beats, she shifted back. "I am truly sorry your friend fell victim to such senseless violence."

"Thanks. I haven't had time to really process it all. I wouldn't be surprised if Rock were attacked at night, like you said. He used to take late walks by himself all the time. He said it was the best time to take a walk because most people were sleeping and the streets were virtually empty. I'd try to warn him but he claimed it was easier to think if he could walk and not be distracted."

"Not good."

"Yeah. Still, I can't figure out why anyone would want to hurt him. He was the gentlest guy I knew. Anyone who really talked to him would know that. Rock wouldn't have been afraid of a mugger. He'd give a mugger money out of pity, so there'd be no need to hurt him. It just doesn't seem right."

The lobby traffic started picking up.

"Dr. Scribe, it can take a long time to accept the death of a loved one. People here have lost so many friends and family that they set up permanent alters to mourn the dead. I understand if you need to take a break. I can come back later or tomorrow if you like."

"I appreciate that. But I have to find out what happened to Rock. He and I would call these situations 'essential pursuits'. There are just certain things you have to do. He sent me an email saying that he found something but didn't tell me what it was. So there's got to be more to this than a mugging. To kill a Rabbi in a church sends a message, no matter who did it. I need to figure out what the message is and I need your help."

Mari winced. "I did not realize your friend was Jewish. This complicates matters. The peace treaty between Egypt and Israel is extremely fragile right now. First Palestine, then Lebanon. Many Egyptians remain upset about the Israeli invasion over the Suez Canal. If news of this murder should spread, it could plunge all of North Africa into a bloody battle for years to come."

Scribe had an expression of pain and exasperation, taking in the cascading waterfall for a moment's relief. He knew Mari was right, but he hadn't come to Cairo to save the world. Had he known Chamberlain's invitation involved any of this, he would have missed his second flight, too. But because of Rockman, Scribe was committed to finding out what happened and helping the police catch the guy who killed his friend.

"Well, that's what I get for taking the free trip to Cairo." Scribe gestured with open palms. "So you'll help?"

Mari frowned with concern. "Why don't you let the police handle this. I know you want to help, but what can you do?"

"Find out what the police know and figure out the rest."

"I'd like to help you, Dr. Scribe, but I don't like dealing with the Cairo police. It's an occupational hazard. They can make it hard for my business."

"I see. Look, all I want to do is make some sense of what happened to Rock and straighten out this business with the students. Mari, if you don't want to help me, that's fine. But I'm going to get to the bottom of this if I have to do it alone."

Mari recalled he had come to visit some exchange students but, until that moment, she'd forgotten. She lifted her beeping phone, checked the text, and cleared the screen.

"Dr. Scribe, keep in mind that the people of Cairo are very similar to those in the United States. They are nationalistic and suspicious of foreigners asking questions. A knowledgeable guide who knows the city and the people will make all the difference."

Scribe bowed like the Dalai Lama. "Thanks Mari. I know you're taking a risk helping me. You have to work and live here after I'm gone so I don't want my snooping around to cause problems for you."

"Dr. Scribe, the biggest problem I see is that this incident could escalate to dire consequences. If I can help to discover what has happened, it is my duty as an Egyptian to do so."

As she transitioned to make a second statement, Mari rested her hand on the back of Scribe's arm. Beyond Scribe's tension from the trip and the news of his friend's death, Mari could feel a subdued strength in his well-developed triceps hidden beneath a long-sleeve shirt.

"Also Dr. Scribe, I've been hired as your guide for the next three days, so technically I am obligated to tour you around the city. Besides, I would like to keep an eye on you to ensure that my gratuity remains safe." She gave Scribe a much bigger smile than Mona Lisa gave Leonardo.

Mari didn't have to help him. But extending herself made an impression. The reaction was both chemical and tangible, an emotional aphrodisiac. Casual inspection found that Mari had moved closer to him during the course of the conversation and she hadn't removed her hand from his arm. The sensation Scribe felt made him hope her meaning matched his interpretation. After a few seconds, he coyly conceded. "Okay, I'll accept your offer to help on two conditions."

A tinge of red entered Mari's cheeks. "What would they be?"

Scribe baritoned, "From this moment forward, you have to call me David."

Playfully nodding she asked, "And the second?"

Scribe returned with a sober expression, "Give me that last shawarma."

EIGHTEEN

Cocoa was in rare form. She wailed on Jack because he was the only person around who'd listen. Rick and Terry volunteered to go out for a walk, but only to escape Cocoa's wrath. Since yesterday's incident, Cocoa seethed that she hadn't yet received a public apology.

According to her version of the incident, Cocoa was actively using her hands to speak. When the conversation got heated, Cocoa brought her hands from her waist to her chin as if to say, "So what!" Unfortunately, the woman interpreted the gesture as an obscenity and spit in Cocoa's face. It took three guys to pin Cocoa against a file cabinet to prevent her from burning down the entire building.

"They don't know me, Jack. I'm from the 'Boogie Down'. I've seen people bleed for less."

Cocoa Santana was a honey colored Latina from Bronx, New York. She was absolutely gorgeous, and she knew it. Even though she had looks to die for, she had a mouth that could kill. Stay on Cocoa's good side and you were in for pleasant conversation with a beautiful woman. But that was almost impossible to do. Most people found themselves unknowingly on her bad side and, by that time, it was too late. The machine gun tongue had begun to fire and the only thing anyone could do was take cover.

Scribe coached Cocoa and Jack on the Debate Team. Jack was clearly his protégé, but Scribe had always found Cocoa compelling and trained her to refute the opposing team's arguments. Her intelligence glowed, but so did her mean streak. Jack was the only one that could bear to be around her for extended periods of time. Not that he liked her ranting, but Scribe suspected Jack's sweet tooth gave him a higher threshold for pain.

"The people in this country are crazy!" Cocoa intoned.

"Cocoa, people here are more expressive than Americans in certain conversations, like politics and personal disagreements."

"Whatever. We were in a business setting and she made it personal. When she started talking that smack about the West having no morals, I stayed cool. But then she shot her mouth off about Bill Clinton being a womanizer? First off Jack, you know Big Willie is my boy. Second, look at the treatment of women in this country. Baskets on their heads dressed in all that hot burlap walking around in hundred degree weather. And she wants to call Clinton a womanizer? Please!"

"I see your point. But we're in a foreign country. There're going to be clashes of culture and differences of opinion." Jack fingered his glasses closer to the bridge of his nose. "You think I like being interrogated about Bush everywhere I go? But I realize I'm representing for a lot of folks back home, so I try to treat it all like stories to tell when I get to the crib. Know what I'm saying? For sure it's crazy, but you gotta try to chill."

"Chill? You act like I'm the one who started it? She stepped way over the line. I'm not laying down for nobody. I hear what you're saying, but didn't the program prep these fools about representing for Egypt?"

Cocoa paced, opening and closing her fists. She continued.

"Okay, there are some cultural differences. But is it right for a forty year old woman to get aggressive with a twenty year old college student in an office setting about politics? I don't think so. So what I'm *not* trying to hear from you, Jack, is some guilt trip about why I should feel bad about getting in her grill; especially when she's disrespecting America."

"How did she disrespect America?"

"Jack, the President of the United States is an institution. Anybody, past or present, holding the office stands for America. To attack a President is to indirectly attack America. That's why former Presidents still have Secret Service agents. So I'm saying, insulting any of our Presidents would symbolize insulting America. We can't have that. Her little 'after the fact' snipe at Clinton was disrespectful to the U.S. Bush 43 isn't my favorite, but he gets respect for holding down the institution."

Jack sighed, equally from fatigue and because Cocoa had a point. Scribe didn't send her into debates to wave the white flag. She would sashay up to the podium like "Fran the Nanny" and let the other team take in her womanly features. After a devious Garfield expression, the next sound was a blistering barrage of phrases resembling Angela Davis in a UFC cage match.

Jack put one foot on the coffee table. "So what did you do next?"

"You know me. I got in her face and told her she'd better back up. She was already close enough to lick me. There's no concept of personal space over here. Anyway, she screams 'There is no shame in America.' I'm like, 'And?' You know I talk with my hands so I threw 'em up and rolled my neck. I even closed my eyes while I did it to dismiss her even more. I sure did."

"Well Cocoa, over here that hand gesture means 'F-You', to put it mildly."

Cocoa stood over Jack, crouching slightly, nearly screaming. "I don't care what it means. Nothing gives her the right to do what she did. Before I had a chance to open my eyes, that…that…*woman* spit between my hands into my face. Now you *know* that mess is unacceptable. On top of all that, I was still talking and some of her spit got in my mouth! I went crazy. Terry and Rick jumped across the desk when they saw me pick up that vase. I was about to put a crown of thorns on her head. She'd better be glad they were holding me."

Ugh, he thought. Jack wiped his lips with the back of his hand while muffling a chuckle. Cocoa looked like a pouty Aztec queen with thick black hair and an airbrushed silhouette. Most days Jack didn't care what she said. He was just glad she said it to him. Today he'd been all ears for a different reason. He heard the whole story from the guys last night, but Cocoa hadn't been ready to talk until now. Jack worked hard to build his standing with her and didn't want to lose it to some other guy while out of position.

He could testify that Cocoa was ordinarily a firecracker looking for trouble, but this time her rage was understandable. Hopefully Scribe could say something at dinner that would calm the situation down.

NINETEEN

The Cairo Police Station had a vastness that made it feel like a maze with no destination or meaning. The sea of desks appeared endless but, ironically, there were very few officers sitting at them. Most Cairo cops spent their days in plain clothes protecting the tourism industry. They also kept the soldiers stationed on the streets honest. Not that there was much a couple of plain clothes cops could do against guys with M-16s, but at least the soldiers never knew who was watching.

Inspector Wahid slouched at his desk reclining in exhausted thought. He hadn't had much sleep lately and this new murder wasn't helping his insomnia. His feet were propped up on a broad hutch that was relatively clear, except for Scribe's bio, Rockman's file, and two telephones. The telephone on the right was closer to Wahid because it was the line that carried all the general business. It was the one he always used and the number he gave out on his business card when investigating crimes.

The second hardly ever rang. It was designated as the emergency phone because everyone who had the number was either highly positioned in the government, connected to someone of that caliber, or one of Wahid's family members contacting him out of desperation. The government calls didn't bother Wahid. It was all in a day's work that an occasional bigwig rang to solicit discretion or extra effort on sensitive matters. But he dreaded the phone ringing and one of his family members was on the other line.

The last time that happened was when four hundred Coptic Christians had a standoff with police trying to force them out of 'St. Mary and the Martyr' Coptic Church, just beyond the city limits of Cairo. The church was historic because it had sheltered Coptic worshippers for hundreds of years and was in a terrible state of disrepair. One day the police chained the doors of the church, claiming the congregants renovated it without government permission.

Egyptian Christians are subject to a centuries-old Ottoman law that requires they obtain permits from the President to build churches or do renovations. Such permits are virtually impossible to secure, which Coptics see as a malicious strategy to oppress their people and their faith. When some priests and their followers broke the lock and occupied the church, hundreds of police surrounded the building. This created a two-day, armed standoff.

Being on the force, Wahid's duty was clear but his loyalty was divided. The inhabitants weren't rebels. They were innocents; women, children, and old men. Thankfully the Coptic Pope sent an emissary who was able to quell the confrontation.

That one ended peacefully. But the previous ring happened when his brother called to tell him that Copts were being murdered on New Year's Day last year in his hometown of El Kodesh. During the trial, the prosecutor produced several witnesses testifying that they heard a Coptic shopkeeper curse Islam in the streets of El Kodesh two days before the violence. The village was 250 miles from Cairo and, by the time Wahid arrived, the three day rampage left twenty-two Copts and one Muslim dead. In addition, 260 Coptic homes and businesses were destroyed. The sole conviction was the shop owner, who received three years of hard labor for insulting Islam.

So when the phone rang this time, the hair on the back of Wahid's neck stood up. The first ring seemed to last for five minutes, but its echo slowly subsided. On the second ring, Wahid cleared his throat to compose himself and dampen the internal panic escaping through his shaking hands. As he picked up the receiver, he could feel it slide slightly down his perspiring palm.

"Inspector Wahid speaking." Pressing the receiver to his ear, nerves tingling in the side of his face.

"Wahid, what have you turned up? I need a solid lead to convince the Police Commission that everything is being handled. I've endured threats all afternoon."

Even though Wahid felt blasted for information he didn't have, he was relieved that it was Chief Habash on the line. Normally, the Chief's anxiety would transfer to him in these situations. Yet, given the dreaded possibilities when that phone rang, Wahid felt relaxed and almost serene.

"No, sir. Nothing yet. Just some information about the fellow that Rockman emailed before his death."

"Well, spit it out."

"Yes sir. It seems that David Scribe is an American professor who is moderately published and respected for his work. He was a colleague of Rockman at the same Westerville University in the United States. We attempted to contact Scribe but he has not yet responded. We think he landed in Cairo two days ago and had access to the victim. Even though it's a stretch, he's the only person of interest we have so far. I'll keep you informed and call the moment I hear from him. Meanwhile, I sent Saba to question the local rabbis. Rabbi Mizrah confirmed that Rockman worshipped at their synagogue for a few months last year, but has not seen him since August. The other rabbis only knew him by name, so they were of little assistance."

"Let me see if I follow you. We have a mysterious rabbi who mysteriously ends up on his back murdered in a church. And his mysterious friend mysteriously hasn't called you back and confessed to being the killer. Is that what you're telling me Wahid?"

"Unfortunately sir, yes."

"Well, the only thing that's not mysterious is what will happen to your job if we don't find the killer and finish this whole business before it gets away from us!"

With a clank on the other end of the receiver, Habash was gone. Wahid's relaxed state wore off as he glanced down at the photos of Rockman's body and wondered about the wound on the inside of Rockman's wrist.

TWENTY

Eleven o'clock meant only two hours had passed since Scribe landed in Cairo. He'd been on so many emotional highs and lows since leaving the States, he felt like a manic depressive stuck inside a yo-yo. After signing in, the officer at the front desk directed Scribe and Mari toward the back of the room. The sparsely spread uniformed cops were typing reports and filing paperwork, the usual. The plain clothes police were tapping each other and pointing. They didn't hide or even try to conceal their stares. It wasn't often that an American visited the station; however, that's not what had their attention.

Mari made her way through the obstacle course of desks and paperweights; deliberate, reserved. From the attention she commanded at the airport, the wide nostrils of the sitting lawmen followed suit. Still something was different about it this time. They were tentative, yet alert. Scribe sensed their hesitant concentration, but half paid attention because he walked ahead of Mari, mentally sizing up the precinct for a nearby exit, just in case.

"Inspector Wahid?"

"Yes."

"I'm David Scribe. I received your message and came to find out how I can help."

Wahid closed the folder, covered it with a phonebook, and rose to shake. "Professor Scribe, thank you for coming. Please have a seat."

"Thank you. Oh, allow me to introduce…" Scribe turned slightly to present Mari. Before he could, he observed a recognition in her eyes.

"Subbah-el-kheir Lamir."

"Good morning to you, Mari. It's been a long time. How are the plays coming?"

"I have one soon to be complete. How is your family?"

"As well as can be." Mari pressed her lips together and nodded.

They all sat and Scribe gave Mari a *'You could have told me you knew him before we got here'* look. She glanced at him curtly and hurried her eyes back to Wahid. Wahid calmly swept Rockman's file and Scribe's bio in his left desk drawer.

Scribe waited with an eager quietness.

"Professor, I regret to inform you that Rabbi Rockman was found murdered early yesterday morning. Let me say that I am sorry for the loss of your friend and we will do everything in our power to see that justice is done."

There. He'd said it. Scribe knew that Rockman was dead, but Wahid's declaration made it seem somehow more real and official.

Scribe bit his bottom lip, tucked both thumbs into his fists, and nodded thank you. His eyes narrowed. "Why would someone do this?"

"We don't know everything, but we think that two nights ago your friend was walking in Old Cairo around midnight and was accosted in an alley. He managed to fight off his attacker long enough to make it into St. George's Church where he was fatally wounded and died shortly thereafter."

"How do you know he was attacked outside first?"

"We found bloodstains at the bottom of the outer staircase that we matched to Rabbi Rockman this morning. Also, the abrasions on his fingertips suggest that he clawed his way up the steps and through the doorway of the church."

Wahid looked matter-of-fact, but nevertheless pleased with himself. "Professor Scribe, do you know why Rabbi Rockman might have been in the Old City so late at night?"

"No. I just learned he was here this morning when I arrived and got your email. All I knew was that he vanished over a year ago from the University. I heard he'd had some kind of fallout with the President about tenure and thought he'd call me after getting resettled; but I never heard from him…until his email."

"So you've not heard from him in a year and he decides to contact you that night?

"Yes."

"I see." Wahid pretended to jot down Scribe's answers, peeking up occasionally.

"Professor, we believe that you may be the last person the Rabbi contacted before he was killed. So anything you can tell me would be helpful. What did his message say?"

"It said that he found something and that he couldn't tell me what it was right then, but he planned to later."

"Is that it?"

"Pretty much."

"Huh." Wahid ran his thumb down the middle of his moustache as he turned things over.

Scribe broke the silence. "Oh, there is one more thing. Did he have a leather flip-over bag with a shoulder strap when you found him?"

"No. But we did notice bruises on his forearms that could have come from something being squeezed and perhaps ripped away from him. The Coroner's office told us about that, but we had nothing to go on until now."

Breaking her long silence Mari added, "It appears that he may have been murdered for whatever was in his case, which may be what he was going to share with Professor Scribe."

Wahid shook his head. "Not the conspiracy theories again, Mari. Pardon me Professor, but all we know is that your friend was killed in a very dangerous part of town where muggings take place all the time. It could simply be a mugging that went too far."

"Maybe, maybe not", Mari fired back. "You are not telling the entire story. Let me see the file and the crime scene photos."

Wahid smarted. "You haven't changed. Always have to be in charge no matter what."

Scribe kept cool while he observed Mari and Wahid joust with verbal lances. Meanwhile, he put two and two together.

Mari smirked at Wahid's remark. "This was not a mugging and you know it."

Relenting, Wahid took a deep breath while clasping his hands and resting his nose on both index fingers. After a second breath Wahid leaned back in his chair.

"Okay. Dr. Scribe, I apologize for the clinical way in which I am about to speak of your friend." Wahid turned to Mari and began. "A priest named Timothy found the body shortly before morning Mass. When we got there, the vic had an ivory-handled dagger lodged into his abdomen. He appeared to be reaching toward the alter with his left hand. Honestly, it seemed like the last place a Jew would be."

"And yet, there he was." Mari chimed in. Wahid's face tightened.

"I don't know if he had been there before that night, but none of the staff acknowledged ever seeing him. Professor, did the Rabbi have any connection to Christianity that you are aware of?"

"Besides an academic one, not really. Rock was a religious historian by training and sort of a mixed metaphor. Everyone that knew him asked the same questions about the way he combined his faith and his work. I still haven't been able to make any sense of it. He was more interested in Jesus than most Christians. But, as an organized tradition, the only religion I've ever known him to participate in is Judaism."

Wahid frowned reflectively. "I understand. That makes this more of a mystery. Not that I'm buying into whatever conspiracy theory you'll eventually make up Mari, but I have to admit that there are some elements here that are abnormal."

"Glad you're admitting something."

Scribe felt like he was eavesdropping on a lover's spat.

"Rabbi Mizrah knew him but not that well. Rockman had been in Cairo for about ten months but left the synagogue after two." Wahid paused before changing direction.

"Professor, could you clear something up for me?"

"Sure", Scribe responded.

"Well, you say you landed this morning, but we have you checked in on a flight arriving two days ago. Explain please."

Scribe stared awkwardly while realizing the implications of the question. "Hey, no way man. Don't even try it. I missed that flight and caught the one that arrived this morning."

Mari chimed in. "I did pick him up this morning and saw him come through customs."

Wahid looked double-teamed. "Were you with him on the flight, Mari? Did you see him deplane?"

"No, Lamir. But I've had his luggage since eight this morning *before* he came in on his flight. I picked it up from the baggage office and the tag says it arrived two days ago."

Wahid wasn't satisfied, but dropped the question. "Professor, how long will you be in Cairo?"

"Through Sunday morning. I'm here to visit our exchange students and attend the Unity Celebration at the Cairo Opera House tomorrow. Our school choir will perform."

"I hear they are quite good."

"They are." *Especially when you consider the abuse they endure from their director*, Scribe thought.

"Professor, if it's not too much trouble, could you send me a copy of Rabbi Rockman's email. I need it for our files." Wahid turned his monitor and handed Scribe the keyboard.

"Lamir, I'm sure Dr. Scribe would be happy to comply after we view the crime scene photos."

Scribe paused, letting their game play itself out.

Drumming his fingers, Wahid stopped abruptly. "Fine."

He produced the top folder from his left drawer, leaving one photo behind. Scribe logged into his account and located Rockman's message.

The pictures were mostly of the dagger. The handle was pearly white, contoured, and carved with gold calligraphy lettering.

Setting the keyboard aside, Scribe inspected the photos. "What's 'Alhamdùlillah'?"

Flipping, Mari didn't look up. "It means 'All praise be to Allah'."

She passed picture after picture of torso shots until Scribe stopped her hand.

"Wait, please." He stared at the expression on Rockman's face and gritted his teeth. “His eyes are pleading.” A tear slid down Scribe’s cheek. He removed his hand from the photo and turned away.

Mari gave Wahid a knowing look and asked, “What’s this in his hand?”

“I think it’s just a shadow or lint on the lens.” Wahid answered.

“No, see how the fingers are bent. He was holding something but these pictures aren’t close enough to make out what it is.

“Oh yeah. He had a piece of string in his hand. It looked to have come from the carpet.”

Mari handed the photos back and waited for Wahid to place them in his drawer. As he did, Scribe forwarded Rockman’s message to Wahid, wiped his face, and turned back to the group.

Wahid took charge. “We’re done here for now. Meanwhile Professor, if you should remember anything else, please contact me. You have one of the best guides in Cairo. I know it will be difficult, but I hope the rest of your stay is pleasant. Please trust that we are working around the clock to bring the killer to justice so, Mari, let us handle it…alone.” Wahid cut his eyes at Mari without turning his face away from Scribe.

“Of course”, Mari replied.

“Oh, Dr. Scribe, one last question.”

Scribe stood behind his chair and Wahid reclined. “When you came in, why didn’t you ask me what happened to your friend? I didn’t tell you any specifics in my message so you could not have known. Yet, when you came in, you merely said you were here to help. Why is that?”

The only thing that came to Scribe’s mind was Gloria the psychic. That wouldn’t play too well against Wahid’s perfectly executed

Columbo question. Mari leaned forward, knowing where this was headed.

Scribe kept a straight face. "You said it was serious and I just assumed the worst."

Mari pursed her lips, then intentionally relaxed.

"Right. Well, in my experience Professor, when a person doesn't ask what happened to the victim, it's usually because they already know."

Mari stepped forward. "Lamir, are you arresting Professor Scribe?"

"No, just thinking out loud."

She pressed. "Then we're done here."

"Almost. Dr. Scribe, again this is just procedure, but I'll have to ask you to surrender your passport until we can verify your arrival date to Cairo."

Scribe flashed to Mari. "Can he do this?"

"I'm afraid so. If you do not, he can detain you."

Scribe handed the blue booklet over and Wahid plucked it from his hand with two fingers.

Tossing the passport in his desk drawer, Wahid rose and spoke in a droll tone. "Shakrun Dr. Scribe, thank you for coming. I am confident that we are close to finding your friend's killer and assure you that you will be the first to know when we do."

TWENTY ONE

The Keeper rose from his slumber with a jolt. Rifling through the leather satchel, he smashed his fist against the stone floor. "*How could they? How could they give this Jew access to the very thing his people forsook? Our brothers died preserving this knowledge! For what? To have it trampled and profaned? The elders have forsaken the way and allowed our ranks to be broken. If there is no shedding of blood, there can be no remission of sin.*

After a few moments of meditation, he rose to gather his shoes and placed the document back into Rockman's bag. While withdrawing his hand, the Keeper rubbed a protruding shape zipped into a side pouch. Tapping the floor produced echoes that came from a hard substance. The reflection of the metallic object was amplified as the early morning sunrays entered the bars of his overhead window.

A picture frame.

I knew it! They are too old to detect his treachery, but they will be made to see.

With that, the Keeper turned and lumbered down the corridor.

When Rick and Terry returned from their walk, they felt heat coming from the door. They had to go in to get dressed for dinner with Scribe, but they didn't want to be blistered by Cocoa's temper.

"You first dude." Rick said, pushing Terry in the small of his back.

Terry looked like one of the Hebrew boys being thrown into the fiery furnace. He leaned back on his heels and braced the doorway with both hands. "Naw, bruh. I'm not going out like that. She's still mad from when we held her down yesterday."

When Cocoa arrived earlier to talk to Jack, Rick and Terry b-lined for the exit. They scatted out of there so fast, they'd forgotten their keys and dreaded knocking. While they scuffled and laughed in the hallway, a gust of cool air swooshed from the apartment catching them by surprise.

"What are you clowns doing out there?"

At that moment, time froze and their names escaped them. The only appropriate monikers seemed to be Laurel and Hardy from the dumbfounded looks on their faces. Rick was pudgy, wore round glasses, and routinely sported t-shirts two sizes too big. Terry had to be the love child of Olive Oil and Skeletor, considering his size zero waist and the fact that he could stick his entire arm up the mouth of a Coke machine and pull down any flavor he wished.

"I'll tell you what you're doing out there." Cocoa had a dry comedic pause before delivering the punch line. "Looking stupid, that's what."

Terry shuffled past her. "You're just sore about yesterday."

Cocoa fired back. "If you guys hadn't got to me first, she'd be sore."

Rick followed. "Yeah, and your face would be all scratched up."

The two guys rolled around laughing on the sofa and slapping each other five.

"Go ahead and laugh. But we'll see who's laughing when I medicate her little spitting problem with a bottle of whup aspirin."

Jack chuckled more than the joke warranted, letting out his captive snickers from Rick's previous cutdown.

Cocoa noted the excess and changed the subject. "So where'd you guys go?"

Feeling strong, Rick answered curtly. "Out."

"Out? Smells like you went to an out-house! Just because we're on summer vacation, Rick, doesn't mean you have to stop using deodorant."

The exchange was predictable. Whenever a woman wanted to wound a man for days she could hit him in either of two places: his private or his armpits. Which one hurt him worse depended on who was around at the time of impact. Kicking his private would evoke sympathy from other males. But harpooning his underarms would encourage men to break ranks and change sides immediately for reasons of self preservation. Jack and Terry laughed knowing that coming to Rick's aid would have meant painting a bull's eye on their own sweat glands.

"I mean, people live here Rick, and you come up in here smelling like that? You ought to be ashamed of yourself."

Rick lifted his arms and alternated sniffs. "I'm not musky. I put on Mitchum before we left."

Cocoa pounced. "No you're not musky, you're funky. There's a difference. Musky is when I smell you. Funky is when I choke on you. I don't know about Mitchum but, next time, try soap."

Rick withdrew, looking bleak and despondent. Terry and Jack saw his expression and laughed harder, holding their diaphragms and begging Cocoa to stop so they could catch their breath.

"Rick, we wouldn't have had this problem if you would've helped me yesterday instead of holding me."

"Terry held you, too." Rick pouted.

"But Terry didn't come in here flapping his lips trying to make a funny. You did. Next time, watch your mouth."

Terry and Jack had tears coming out of their eyes and held up both hands wheezing, "No more, please."

Cocoa obliged. "Okay, I'll leave you boys to get ready for dinner, but Rick, please don't forget our little talk on hygiene."

Before Rick could utter a sound, Cocoa had shut the door and was gone. Jack and Terry slid down the sofa onto the floor in deep, silent laughter.

TWENTY TWO

Exiting the precinct, Scribe overcame his reticence and started, "Mari, when were you going to tell me that you and the Inspector were a couple?"

"We are not lovers."

"But you used to be?"

"Only one date, no more. I worked here until two years ago."

Scribe wasn't surprised, but he was relieved. "As a cop?"

"Yes. I have a Master's Degree in Criminology from the American University here in Cairo. I was the lead detective at the time and number one for solving difficult homicide cases. But the bureaucracy decided they did not want a woman being second in command; so I was passed over for a qualified, but less deserving, colleague."

"Wahid."

"Exactly. After which I resigned from the force and pursued my passion for theater. I have written three mystery plays that are based on actual events, but none have received much acclaim. Forgive me for not divulging my acquaintance with Lamir, but he is connected to a part of my life that I have tried to forget."

"So why are you working as a tour guide?"

"The same reason everyone works a job that has little to do

with their passion: money. It also affords the opportunity for me to explore new characters and stay current through the people I meet. In this way, you could call being a tour guide 'research' for my theatrical productions."

"I see. Well, what you don't know about me is that if I weren't a professor I would love to be a detective like Sherlock Holmes. Danger and intrigue tempered by the power of reason—that's living. It's always been profound to me that Sir Arthur Conan Doyle was a believer in spiritualists while his creation, Sherlock Holmes, would regard such ideas as rubbish."

"Perhaps Doyle was working out his own skepticism in Holmes. Yet there are times when Holmes admitted the possibility of the supernatural, even if he didn't believe in it."

"Mari, I'm impressed. You know your Holmes."

"So does that mean I get a break on Lamir?"

"I guess, if you let me read one of your plays."

Unlocking the door, Mari laughed. "You must be an only child."

"How do you know?"

"Because you're always bargaining for something but risking nothing of your own."

Scribe harrumphed and hopped into the passenger side. Saba followed four car lengths back.

"Since we are playing the questions, how *did* you know your friend was dead? It would be against policy, but I assumed Lamir told you…until ten minutes ago."

"Promise you won't laugh again?"

"Yes." Mari alternated between Scribe and the road.

"Okay, here goes. On my outbound flight from the U.S., I met a woman named Gloria. She told me Rock died recently and is trying to tell me something. She was so convincing that I sort of believed her. When I got Wahid's message, I knew."

Mari mulled it over. "She was a sensitive?"

"If you mean a medium, I guess so. She said she could see Rock standing next to me. Only he couldn't talk. He could only make gestures."

"David, the ancient Egyptians believed that the soul remained in the physical realm for a period of time after death."

"The 'Ka'?"

"No, the 'Ba'. 'Ka' is the creative or intellectual power. It is not the soul. 'Ka' is more akin to your word 'spirit' that remains with you until death and then returns to the source of all things. 'Ba' is closer to 'soul' or essence in the West."

"I've read something like that in the Tibetan Book of the Dead."

"Yes, they likewise believe the soul remains with the body for at least three days before moving on."

"Do you believe in this, Mari?"

"I believe that I have seen a lot of things and that anything is possible."

"I guess you're right. I used to feel that Rock and I were Doyle and Holmes trying to figure out who had the right perspective. The problem was that there were always compelling reasons to see us as both right and both wrong."

"That's another reason figuring out why your friend was killed means so much to you. It could move you closer to understanding why your life has taken the path it has."

"I suppose it could. You're not working for my mom, are you?"

Mari giggled.

"Mari, I must admit I feel fortunate to have a tour guide that was the best criminal detective in Cairo."

"As you should." She giggled again.

"Don't take this the wrong way, but you're exactly who I need right now. It sure does seem to score one for the Doyle side. I don't know, but I feel like I've almost been led to the right people and opportunities in my life. But it's still cloudy and I wonder what it all means."

"Then let's figure it out. I do not know the meaning either. But I do know that the trail gets colder every second we lose."

Gesturing for Scribe to put on his seatbelt, Mari added, "And don't worry, I took it the right way."

TWENTY THREE

Father Timothy sat fixated upon the crucified Christ as the wall of candlelight flickered in the background. He had seen plenty of dead bodies in St. George's during the two years since being appointed to the clerical staff, but never on the floor in the aisle. The young priest searched the serene expression of his tortured Savior for solace.

"So much carnage, Lord. So much killing. How could this happen in your house?"

The massive globed dome of St. George's is arguably the most recognizable landmark in Old Cairo. It is one of the few round churches that still exist in the East and its circular shape is derived from the fact that it is built atop a Roman tower. A robust set of stairs lies hewn along the wall of the tower leading up to the church.

Every stride pained Scribe because he thought of Rockman crawling to a cruel death along this very path. To break his mood, Scribe snapped his head back and viewed the large relief of St. George emerging from the winding brickwork of the outer tower. That image of a Roman soldier on an Arabian stallion spearing a dragon was world famous. He wished Rockman had access to a weapon when he needed it.

Mari's question reaffirmed her presence. "Do you like the relief?"

After a few more steps, Scribe spoke. "It's pretty impressive. Must have taken years to complete."

"Yes. It was all carved by hand. St. George is widely regarded as the warrior-saint of the East, which might explain his appeal to many followers of Christianity and Islam."

Scribe took a chance and asked a taboo question. "What's your take on religion, Mari?"

Mari heisted, as if gathering her thoughts, but instead used the time to decide what kind of answer she would give.

"I live in a Muslim country. So if anyone asks, I am Muslim. But my 'take', as you say, is that people are looking for solutions to problems. If they find something that solves a problem, they use it. Religion solves the problem of meaning for some, so some use it for its practical value."

Mari ended her statement with "Hmmm."

"What?", Scribe inquired.

She smiled and responded. "I have surprised myself. I must feel comfort with you because, in my line of work, telling people what you really think can be costly."

Scribe clasped his hands. "Thank you for sharing." He raised his head and continued. "And I see your point. Most people are doing their best to be happy given what they've been taught. Sure, I get that. But, at the same time, most of the wars we fight have religious undertones; so we could say that religion causes more problems than it solves."

"We could. But it is a matter of perspective."

Scribe thought, *Note to self: Agree to disagree*, as they continued their climb.

When Scribe and Mari finally reached the top of the staircase, they rubbed the backs of their thighs and staggered toward the doorway. The laptop strap hung like an albatross around Scribe's neck. He wondered if this was his climb of penance for missing the first flight. *If only I'd gotten here two days ago.*

Mari's phone beeped. "I need to take this call. Go ahead and look around and I'll meet you in a minute."

From the threshold, Scribe observed tourists inspecting the back of the venerable sanctuary. Some said prayers, some wandered in captivation, some just sat. As soon as he stepped through the doorway, Scribe was drawn to an enormous support column around which three groups were clustered. There was the camcorder group that all talked at once while filming the same icon from five different angles. Then there was the Minolta group snapping pictures and being scolded by an attendant for ignoring the signs forbidding flash photography. And there was the group of children playing tag in the midst of the other two. Scribe took a seat on the pew adjacent to their rosy pillar.

St. George's had the special privilege of housing one of the oldest surviving Black Madonna carvings in the world. The figure was not particularly detailed, but was nevertheless protected in a tubular, bullet-proof casing that encouraged tourists to circumambulate as if it were the Black Stone of Mecca. Hundreds of these representations could be found, mostly in Europe, depicting both Mary and the infant Jesus with dark pigment. It didn't surprise Scribe that one was on display in Africa, but it rather amazed the people pressed against the glass.

The sculpture was a Romanesque, dark wood carved in the 11th or 12th century. The seated woman boasted high cheekbones, large hands, thick lips, and big brown eyes. The child had similar features, low cropped hair, and held a box in his left hand. Both looked straight ahead, lacking the downcast lowliness for which Christ and Mary were famous.

"You also like the Black Madonna, I see?" Mari slid into the pew next to Scribe.

"Yes. I like the legends about her."

"You mean as both Mary and Isis?"

"Those and the one that says she's the daughter of Jesus."

"I've never heard that one, David. What is it?"

Scribe put his arm around the back of the pew, whispering while he leaned. "Remember that business with Jesus and Mary Magdalene that had everyone in an uproar?"

"Um hmm."

"Well there, Magdalene is smuggled from Palestine to southern France while pregnant. In this story, she comes through Egypt with her young daughter on her way to France, and is helped by the same people who hid the Holy Family from King Herod."

Mari cupped Scribe's ear. "The crypt where Jesus and his parents stayed is right below here inside a small, Coptic Orthodox church named St. Sergius. Roman soldiers looking for them walked the streets above many times and never knew." She turned again to listen.

"So I guess you know who helped to hide him?"

Mari nodded.

"This supposedly explains why the Copts had one of the first churches and oldest Christian crosses. The legend says that Magdalene brought Christ's teachings to them while they hid her and her dark-skinned daughter, Sara. These guardians, or Keepers as they were called, suggested that Magdalene disguise Sara as her servant for safety."

Mari smarted. "Even if this happened, it doesn't mean the girl was Jesus' daughter."

"True. And nowhere in the story does Magdalene ever say that Sara is Jesus' child."

"So where does that come from?"

"Well, the legend says that the Keepers helped them because Sara looked and acted like the toddler they'd sheltered thirty years prior."

Mari loved a good tale. Clearing her throat in thought she said, "If this is so, then the Copts had contact with three generations of the Holy family, which adds much to their stature in the Christian faith."

"Exactly. But the Catholics aren't much on sharing power, so Rome never officially recognized the Coptic role in sheltering Jesus or anyone else. Anyway, the story goes on to say that Magdalene and Sara make it to southern France, she becomes known as 'Sara la Kali' or 'Sara the Black', and is adopted as the patron saint of the Gypsies for her charitable work... hence the title: The Black Madonna."

Scribe winked. "Maybe you can add that to your tour information and send me a share of the tips."

After a muffled snicker, Scribe remembered Rockman. "Where do you think we can find Father Timothy?"

Mari understood his shift in tone. "Probably in the monastery. It is connected to the church by that front hallway."

Mari led Scribe down a left aisle while he surveyed the pictorial re-enactment of St. George slaying the dragon. The murals were aged, but well-preserved, and the colors remained vibrant against the setting of stained glass windows and hardwood floors. The chapel seemed to be an updated blend of many eras mixing crystal chandeliers, teak wood floors, and old-world Lebanese cedar railings with supporting balusters expertly crafted from Egyptian cyprus. With each step, Scribe had a greater awareness that he was walking in an elevated environment because each stride conveyed the sensation of being in a floating house. For some people, this brought awe and wonder. For Scribe, it brought the creeps.

The corridor was tight and dark, barely wide enough for two people to pass. It remained dimly lit on the sides by candles so thick they could burn for a month without being replaced.

Scribe stayed two paces behind Mari, murmuring. "Would safety lighting destroy the integrity of the building?"

"The foundation of the structure dates back to the seventh century. Because of its age, the decision was made not to update the lighting in the hallway for fear of damaging the original stone. Also, some of the older priests thought that since the corridor leads from the sanctuary to the monastery, it represents the passage from darkness to light in either direction. For that reason, the younger priests arguing for practicality were dismissed as not appreciating the value of tradition."

Scribe chortled. "Darkness to light? More like healthy to injured. Usually I respect my elders but I have to go along with the underlings on this one."

Silence from Mari conveyed to Scribe that the signals from women were the same around the world after a man spoke: smile good, silence bad.

Emerging from the hallway, they found themselves in an anteroom also accessible from the chapel.

Why didn't she bring me that way? Scribe thought. The double door to the chapel loomed to their far right as if it were made for a priest named Goliath.

"The door is cedar wood and stands seven meters high. No one quite knows why it is adorned with animal figures, although they are quite intricate. My tours remark that the entryway is lovely but imposing. I always reply that if you expected the biggest man in the universe to come by for a visit, you would make sure he could get in the door." Scribe gave a courtesy chuckle.

Besides the door, the anteroom had tasteful, yet basic, furnishings with the feel of Don Corleone's foyer in *The Godfather*. By design, the room led to a much larger inner chamber where the faithful came to petition St. George for help and blessings. On the north wall hung a sea of candles culminating in the exalted figure of a crucified Christ. On the south wall, they spotted a lone figure huddled in the corner and clad with an iron collar wrapped about his neck.

"Mari, is he kissing that chain?"

"Yes. It is said to have been used in the torture of St. George. According to the faithful, whoever places the halter of the chain around the neck, winds the chain around the body, and offers prayers to St. George will be in a state of grace. It is also said that those suffering from incurable maladies confined in the chain for three days have been known to recover."

Scribe leaned in. "Well, that would explain why people of many religions come here to pray. It goes along with your theory, too. Whatever works, no matter what you call it or how bizarre it seems, right? Rome has St. Peter's chain and Egypt has St. George's."

"Correct."

Scribe continued. "He doesn't look like he wants to be bothered, but I've got to find Father Timothy."

"Okay." Mari led Scribe over and briefly spoke with the man in his native language. Afterwards the rotund captive turned toward

Scribe and said, “Dr. Scribe, I am sorry for your friend’s death. I find him this morning in chapel and have been here since la Policia left.”

“Father Timothy?”

“Yes.”

Timothy was visibly shaken, a mixture of sorrow, penance, and frailty.

Scribe spoke slowly with a kind demeanor. “I know this is hard for you and I’m terribly sorry, but could you tell me if you saw anything that could help us figure out what happened to my friend?”

“I told Inspector everything I saw. He took a few pictures before other officers come.”

Mari’s wheels turned. “He took his own pictures?”

“Yes, with pocket camera.” Timothy lifted his hand and the chain to mime snapping a Polaroid.

She knelt down. “Did he take any close up photos?”

“Yes, of knife in Rabbi’s belly and of his hand.”

Neither of them had to ask. They knew Wahid had been hiding something. Now they were closing in on it.

“What about his hand?”, Scribe pressed.

“Rabbi had hole in his right wrist and clutching string of beads like rosary in left. Beads wrapped around middle three fingers. Had the letters:

COSM

Timothy slumped over praying. “How could it be in this holy place?”

Scribe heard footsteps in the shadows. “Who’s there?” Mari looked but saw nothing.

“Mari, I just figured something out.”

“What?”

"I'll tell you in the car." Father Timothy was calling on St. George and didn't hear them walk away.

An enshrined silver icon of St. George fighting a dragon stood near the mouth of the hallway. It looked like an elaborate telephone booth where visitors could kneel under soft light before an etching of their patron saint.

As they passed, a bony grip weakly seized Scribe's shirt. He remained startled even after realizing that an elderly nun with bent posture stood urgently tugging at his waist.

"I see much danger around your aura, my son. Be careful." With that, she melted back into the shadows beneath the felt of a magenta wall cover.

Mari gave Scribe a 'What was that all about?' stare. Scribe shrugged and grabbed her hand. Opting against the dark corridor, he double-timed toward a rear, sunlit staircase. Noting the courtyard below, he figured Mari's van could be reached quickly and with few onlookers or threats. Scribe couldn't decide if it was the nun's warning, Rock's death, or an independent wariness, but he suddenly had an urgent feeling against being at St. George's.

As they descended the outer steps and neared the bottom, a voice faintly cried out behind them, "Dave!"

Scribe broke their stride to look back. Seeing no one, he turned to resume when...*Crash!* Something exploded at the base of the staircase. Snapping around, Mari saw a hideous sight. Something lie mangled and twisted five feet in front of them, legs and vertebrae bent backwards from the impact. Hooked to its belt loop was a golden police shield and an empty revolver holster. Mari made out the features of the creature's blood-soaked face. *Saba*.

She ordered, "Run!"

Mari clutched Scribe's hand and they sprinted, zigzagging to avoid the ricocheting ping of bullets denting the cobblestone. They couldn't see the shooter, but whoever it was sat perched in a high place; only missing by inches. Judging from the angle of the gunfire, their only hope was to run back to the wall near Saba's oozing body.

Diving, they inched along the surface toward Mari's Vinta. They'd parked out back and the only people around were beggars who'd also run for cover when Saba torpedoed to the ground. Millimeters separated their toes from being ripped off by the mushrooming surface of hollow point shells.

In the adrenaline rush, Mari slipped and fell on her backside, mouth agape and looking up. A hooded figure pointed a standard issue .357 squarely between her eyes. She knew firsthand that the ammunition it held had a lead core jacketed in steel and would expand upon impact. It was designed to be accurate and provide greater resistance to crosswind deflection. Because of this, she also knew that if this guy landed a round anywhere near her face, she was toast.

It all happened so fast. Mari almost cried when she opened her eyes. Scribe had snatched her by the arm that covered her face just in time. His sacrifice was a graze that tore the sleeve of his favorite shirt, but he'd live...and so would Mari. Locked in each other's embrace, they didn't realize the shots had ended until the blaring sirens moved closer. The pointing and shrieking of gathering bystanders served as their cue to dash for the Vinta and burn rubber.

TWENTY FOUR

Scribe and Mari waited for the students to arrive. They were scheduled for an early dinner at the Birdcage, a five-star Thai restaurant on the second floor of the Semiramis.

The drive over had been awkward and quick, filled with anxious chatter that served the function of allowing their heart rates to decrease more than anything else. Scribe could see that Mari was shaken and he didn't know if it was about her head almost being blown off or Saba balled up like a pretzel drenched in ketchup. Either way, he decided to let her have a minute to regroup after asking if she was okay.

Scribe went up to his room and cleaned his cut. For time's sake, he changed his shirt and threw on a dinner jacket instead of putting on a suit before joining Mari. Her prêt a porte outfit came in handy as usual. When Scribe approached, Mari pressed 'send' and slipped her phone onto her lap.

"Boyfriend?" Smalltalk was the most polite thing he could think of while sitting down.

"No boyfriend; just rearranging other clients."

More information than he asked for. That was a good sign. Scribe shook his head and smirked slyly.

Mari returned the gesture. "So what about your family?"

"I don't have one now." Mari could tell it was something sad.

"How long?"

"Three years"

"I'm sorry."

"Me, too. Thanks." Scribe took a sip of water. "So who was that guy and why was he shooting at us?"

"I don't have a clue. When I fell, I saw that he had a dark cloak and a .357 in his right hand. The bullets were hollow points, standard police issue, but anyone could get their hands on them. The gun must have jammed or I wouldn't be sitting here now." She reached for a knife and spread butter on a wheat roll with sesame seeds.

"Well, thank God for jams." He passed the fruit jellies to Mari, waiting on her reaction.

She passed on his pun, with a soft look. "Sometimes God has help, so thank you, too." Scribe didn't see that one coming. Recognizing the discomfort of his blush, Mari spread the coat of marmalade generously.

Scribe shifted the subject. "Do you think that cop was with the shooter?"

"Not unless they met up at the church."

"Why's that?

"Because Saba tailed us from the police station. I saw him in the rearview mirror a few car lengths behind. We trained together at the Academy and all those years on the job stay ingrained in the instincts. In addition, I know Lamir."

"Why didn't you tell me?"

"We are also trained to know when our cover has been compromised. I thought you may have reacted and tipped him off."

"Alright." Scribe gave her an 'I'm not dumb' flash of his teeth.

"If that's the case, then we either had two guys trying to kill us when one slipped and busted his melon. Or..." He hesitated, recognizing that he hadn't asked if Saba was a friend or simply a co-worker.

"Or...?" Mari reiterated, urging him to go on.

"Or", Scribe risked, "we could have one guy trying to kill us who bench pressed Saba and sent him bungee jumping without a cord."

A tad more graphic, but essentially the same theory Mari entertained. In response, she showed him that women invented the art of subject switcheroo.

"So what did you figure out at St. George's before we left Father Timothy?" Her shifting color eyes more inquisitive than her words.

Scribe appreciated her train of thought. "First, let me ask you, is Wahid a Copt?"

"Yes. How did you know?"

"The hands."

She nodded slowly, waiting for the blanks to be filled in.

"I noticed the small blue crucifix tattooed on the inside of his right wrist, a well known symbol of the Coptic faith around the world."

"I have seen that, but I thought it was a personal thing."

"I think it's connected to all this."

"How?"

"Well, Father Timothy said Rock had a hole in his right wrist. Call me crazy, but I'm willing to bet a blue crucifix tattoo was there before someone dug it out."

Mari let that soak in.

Scribe followed his thought. "I already know how it sounds, especially since Rock didn't have one when I knew him. But it seemed like more than a coincidence to have Wahid on my mind when I learned about the hole in Rock's wrist. It was as if my mind lit up and something guided me toward the connection."

Mari pursed her lips. "But your friend was a Rabbi."

"True, but he was no ordinary Rabbi. I wouldn't be surprised if he were involved in other things."

Mari had heard of Jews for Jesus, so this could be like that. But instead of narrowing the list of suspects, the list got wider.

She finally spoke. "So the killer could be a zealous Muslim, implied by the dagger, or an enraged Jew who felt betrayed, or…". She stopped short.

Scribe took the baton. "Or…a disgruntled Copt…or should I say 'cop'?"

"You don't think Lamir did this?" Mari bowed her neck. "David, Lamir is sometimes a jerk but he's not a murderer."

"Maybe not. But he didn't tell us about the hole in Rock's wrist and he lied to us about the beads."

"I know. I've been thinking about those beads since Father Timothy mentioned them. Maybe Lamir didn't want to tip his hand, but it's definite that he's hiding something."

Scribe scooted his chair closer to the table. "If Wahid didn't do it, it's possible he's protecting the murderer because he knows who it is or there is a religious connection."

Mari responded. "Whatever your friend found is probably the motive for his death. That's why Lamir wanted the email transmission."

"Either way, Mari, I had my doubts about Inspector Wahid at the precinct. That's why I left off the attachment when I forwarded the message."

He was one of the few Christians on the job, and he took pride in it. Wahid didn't wear his faith on his sleeve, but he knew his presence on the force meant more than being a police officer. It meant hope that Egypt would embrace multiculturalism in the same way the world had embraced Egypt as the cradle of civilization. Still his climb had been slow and rough.

Christians, in general, are constantly harassed in Egypt. Among them, Catholics are given much more deference in society because of their relationship with the Vatican. They have worldwide support as the popular 'brand' of Christianity and, of course, Catholicism is the richest tradition with the most followers. Next in line are an assortment of Protestants, mainly foreign missionaries who do more humanitarian work than anything else. By far those suffering the greatest religious persecution are the indigenous Christian population in Egypt, the Coptics.

Coptic comes from the word 'Hikaptah', one of the ancient names for Memphis, Egypt's first capital. When used religiously, it specifically refers to Egyptian Christians. Copts, as they are called, have a Pope too; but he doesn't enjoy the status of his Catholic counterpart. Thus, in Muslim Egypt, Copts are worse than third class citizens—they are second class Christians.

Despite millions of members, the disrespect towards Copts is pervasive. Copts comprise almost 15 percent of Egypt's population, yet have no seats in the People's Assembly. While the government pays the salaries of Muslim Imams out of public funds, Copt priests are relegated to scrounging up support from their poor congregants. Moreover, Islam is the official state religion. That means Copts that proselytize are subject to arrest. Knowing all of this made Wahid feel that he had the weight of his community on his shoulders every time he showed up for work. Due to the lack of Copts in the army, he feared that if this incident were made an international one, Copts would become Egypt's Lee Harvey Oswald.

Scribe's arrival time had checked out, but why had he deleted the attachment from the Rabbi's email? Wahid had no idea what Scribe was trying to hide until he got the call about Saba. The area was taped off and barricaded by squad cars to keep out curious onlookers. All witnesses had been questioned before Wahid arrived.

A rookie officer approached with the informal briefing. "Inspector, no one saw Scribe do it, but they all place him and Mari at the scene near the body and fleeing once sirens were heard."

"Indo, I never should've sent him."

Officer Indo allowed his silence to swallow Wahid's comment. "Sir, the crowd is growing. What should we tell them?"

"Nothing now. They'll find out soon enough. But I'm sure they won't be too concerned that a police officer was murdered."

Indo ground his teeth. "Saba was a good cop and a good Muslim."

"I know. I have to find a way to tell his wife. They both groaned.

"Inspector, the man next to the rail also said he heard shots fired but he didn't see the shooter. Ballistics found some spent shell casings that could've come from Saba's weapon. There were a few drops of blood near one of the rounds, so one of the suspects may be wounded."

"Indo, I want every available officer to dragnet this city and find those two today."

"Understood." Indo exhaled and then resumed. "Sir, let me help hunt this guy down. I know I'm still fresh, but it's the least I can do."

Wahid nodded. "Just stay on top of this scene and I'll let you know when I need you. And bring me those shell casings. I want to take a look at them."

“Right away, sir. Oh Inspector, should I notify Chief Habash?”

It’s not that Wahid didn’t like Habash. He didn’t. The main problem was that he didn’t like working for Habash. But that’s where he had been for the last twenty years. So he had to be a team player, or at least appear to be at this point.

Wahid gave Indo a measured shake of the head. “No, I’ll tell him myself.”

TWENTY FIVE

The atmosphere of The Birdcage sizzled like the food being prepared in the open air kitchen. The designer obviously loved fountains because frescos with invisibly audible water drips created a tropical ambience. Scribe wondered if a better name for the restaurant would have been The Amazon. Smells of cooking oils and vegetables blended with the crackling of the live band. The hotel had succeeded in melding a hint of the exotic into the midst of vintage wine racks and world class etiquette from the servers.

"At least somebody knows how to treat a lady", Cocoa purred as the Maitre D' held her chair while she sat.

"Thank you."

"You are quite welcome ma'am. If there is anything you desire, my name is Ali and I am at your service." Smiles exchanged before Ali returned to his post.

"Cocoa, glad to see you're in good spirits."

"Good to see you Professor. You know a sister can work the room anywhere in the world."

Jack didn't react. Terry and Rick held their breath.

"Cocoa, fellas…I'd like you to meet Mari. She's been my guide since I landed and she also writes plays. She used to be a police officer."

"Hello everyone." All the boys, including Jack, were enamored by the way her dark hair fell around her mouth when she crinkled her nose. Looking at Jack, Cocoa half rolled her neck. Scribe sipped his water with a grin.

"Then maybe she can arrest that fool who disrespected me at the office." Cocoa recounted the story blow by blow while the waiter brought drinks. Rick and Terry acted out how they jumped across their desks to keep Cocoa out of jail.

"If I don't get a personal apology from a diplomat, there's going to be some kicking and screaming around here…and I plan to do all the kicking. They need to bring me what's in those bottles on the rack, 'cause these people get on my nerves. No offense, Mari."

"None taken." Mari watched Cocoa and enjoyed the free expression. Women had to stick together, no matter the culture. Mari's easy tone and demeanor conveyed to Cocoa that she was no rookie in female to female public interaction.

Scribe tried to change the tenor of the conversation. "Cocoa, I'm only authorized to buy food, no alcohol. Besides, there's enough booze in the sauce to make you tipsy all night." The whole table laughed.

The evening specialties were garlic pepper shrimp, cashew chicken, and crispy rice in peanut sauce.

Cocoa fanned at Scribe as the waiter made his second approach. "Hey, tell them to bring me the shrimp 'cause I don't want no nuts in my food."

Raucous laughter erupted and other patrons stared. Ali winked at Cocoa and turned his back. Jack's cheekbones tensed.

As is custom, the Maitre D' brought them to the lounge for after-dinner tea, pastries, and conversation. Scribe pulled Jack aside.

"Jack, I need a favor."

"Whatchu got Doc?"

"It's a long story but I need you to translate a text for me."

"What language?"

"Greek. Can you do it?"

"Can I do it? Do grits make grocery? Does bacon make grease? Where is it?" In addition to being captain of the debate team, Jack was a Poli Sci major with a minor in Philosophy. He grew up between Chino and Moreno Valley with his grandparents and worked hard to win a scholarship to Westerville. Determined to be a world traveler, Jack taught himself many languages in his spare time. But his knowledge of Greek came from an early desire to be a minister before hard knocks, shady preachers, and intellectual pursuit drove his faith over the edge.

"I'll email it to you now. How long will it take to translate?"

Jack shrugged. "Depends on how long it is. But as soon as I'm finished I'll shoot it back to you."

Scribe stuck out his hand. "Take care of me here, Jack, and I'll do my best on the Cocoa situation. By the way, how's the chase coming?"

"You know me Doc, always got my game face on. Brothers in the Middle East don't have a thing on me." They did the guy hug.

Before pulling away, Scribe spotted Mari rushing over from the window. "David, we have to go."

Bewildered, Jack scanned their faces. "Prof, you alright?"

Scribe followed Mari toward the kitchen, looking back. "I'm good. Just handle that situation as fast as you can."

"Will do."

By the time Wahid and his men reached the sitting room of the

Birdcage, Scribe and Mari were down an alley and blending into the streams of tourists in a nearby souk. Even though it was open-air, it was a good choice. The merchants put their tribal disputes on hold to market their surplus goods, so the police would have a lot to answer for if they upset business by barging through the crowd waving weapons.

Mari dragged Scribe with her voice. "We should be safe here for a while. Just keep moving."

Weaving through the throngs took focus given Mari's pace. Scribe thought holding her hand would be nice for a couple of reasons. Yet foreign men touching local women in an Old City marketplace was not the kind of publicity they needed right now.

Mari ducked into a shop of rugs and yanked Scribe into a side passageway.

"This is why it pays to have a guide, David. There is a souk within the souk where locals shop at local prices."

It was true. Scribe saw no shopkeepers bringing beverages to tourists or anyone speaking at all. Egyptian women browsed leisurely while merchants read newspapers or joked in conversation. The goods were different as well. They were mostly cheap, American brand appliances, knock off Tupperware, and toys.

It made Scribe wonder about the worth of the trinkets people spent so much money on just a few yards away. "Where are we going?"

"We're here." Mari stopped short at a corner booth. A lanky man sat in sandals and wore traditional Muslim garb over a pair of worn tweed slacks.

"As-Salamu Alaykum Uncle Rashim."

"Mari! Salaamu." Rashim set down his tea and embraced Mari thrice, kissing her lightly on alternate cheeks each time.

"Uncle this is David, a friend of mine. He needs a change of clothes and a hat."

"Give an old man a minute. I have fasted all day and my tea has kept me company. But for you, Mari, anything. Good price for your friend, too."

"A thousand thanks, Uncle. We're in a hurry."

Rashim paused. "I have not seen you in six months and you're in a hurry? Do you have Egyptian pounds?" He looked at Scribe.

Shrugging, Scribe shook his head.

"You bring an American here with no money and ask for clothes? Allah, what is this generation coming to?" He mumbled in Arabic, turned his back, and rummaged through the caps and garments.

Scribe leaned over. "What's he saying?"

"He says the least I can do is find a nice Muslim boy and give him strong babies." Scribe kept quiet on what he determined was a crossfire insult.

In two minutes, Scribe donned a striped, button-down kaftan over his trousers and a matching kufi. Nothing fancy or rich, but the perfect outfit for melting into a sea of ordinary Cairo citizens; except for his laptop. Despite the adrenaline rush of the moment, he liked being inconspicuous.

At home, Scribe was notoriously 'unfamous' on purpose. He enjoyed a sense of camouflage instead of bustling with society. His life was so incognito that the word didn't quite capture the way he lived. Scribe generally liked people and garnered a lot of attention from the opposite sex, but rarely acted upon it. It was a sort of intentional non-involvement with others. He did have a few friends he enjoyed catching up with every now and then. Only he hadn't seen most of them in three years or so; not since the accident.

"I'll pay you next week Uncle, I promise."

Rashim waved his hand in protest. “You never pay since you were a girl. You eat all the cakes and drink the tea. You pay me in laughter and kisses. This is good enough.”

“Thanks Uncle.”

“Thank you, sir”, Scribe chimed, waving. Rashim raised his chin and split his gaze between Scribe and Mari and, again, spoke in Arabic.

Heading down another row of shops Scribe asked, “What did he say when we were leaving?”

Mari snickered. “He said for me to come alone next week because he would have a nice Muslim boy waiting with two million camels.”

TWENTY SIX

Back at The Birdcage Cocoa cooperated with Wahid, Bronx style.

"I don't need to calm down. I just don't appreciate you running up in here waving a pistol while I'm having dinner. That's why I don't like cops. Y'all don't respect people's privacy." She finished, staring at Wahid without blinking.

"I truly apologize, madam, but we're conducting a murder investigation."

"Who got murdered?"

"A fellow officer and another Westerville professor, Matthew Rockman." Rick and Terry moved in closer.

Cocoa replied. "I saw him around campus a few times last year. That's wild, but why are you chasing Dr. Scribe?"

"He's a suspect."

"Of what? You think he did it? Man, you're tripping." Wahid glanced at Ali for a translation. Ali's eyes widened and he shook his head.

Cocoa continued. "Besides, Rockman was Scribe's boy. You don't take out your boys."

"Perhaps. But I have witnesses that place him at the scene of the police officer's murder. That officer was 'my boy', as you say, so I intend to find his killer tonight."

"I hear you." Cocoa nodded her head quickly, understanding. "I'm sorry about your man and all, but you got it wrong Inspector *Wahid*." She dragged out the syllables of his name. "Scribe ain't no killer. He's good people."

Wahid surveyed the room. He knew he couldn't arrest an American exchange student in a five-star restaurant for rolling her neck, but he wanted to.

Cocoa saw his hesitation and took another swing. "Since you have nothing better to do with your time, why don't you handcuff that chick who spit on me yesterday at the office? You almost had to come and get *me*." Rick and Terry lowered their heads. A uniformed officer spoke briefly with Ali, then hustled over to Wahid.

"No sign of them anywhere, Inspector. They must have gone into the souk."

"Take twenty men and sweep it. Mari knows the area well. She practically grew up in there."

The officer retorted. "Is she helping the Professor?"

"We'll have to assume so until we find them. I don't see any other way he could've evaded us so long."

Cocoa broke in. "I see why Mari quit."

Wahid followed her words. "What did you say?"

Cocoa repeated her statement, adding emphasis with her hands on her hips. "I said I see why Mari quit."

Wahid leaned in and his voice dropped a decibel. "Why is that?"

"Cause she don't like working with punks." Wahid glared. He didn't know what she meant by 'punk', but it didn't sound good. Cocoa glared back. Rick and Terry came along side and escorted her to the pastry table.

After a few seconds Wahid shifted his gaze away from her back and spotted a dark-skinned man with glasses, wearing red from head to toe, sitting in the corner, and tapping a small electronic device.

Wahid approached. "Who are you?"

The young man answered. "Jack."

"Are you a Westerville student?"

"Yep. Who's asking?"

"Inspector Wahid, Cairo Police." Jack raised his head when Wahid flashed the badge but went back to the screen before it was replaced.

"What are you working on?"

"Wait a minute. I'm almost done. And…send. Voila. Couple of hours? Only took me a couple of minutes."

"What?" Wahid seemed to be both amazed by Jack's declaration and inquiring about its meaning.

Jack couldn't tell which interpretation was correct, but the urgency in Wahid's tone dampened his euphoria. Feeling the stares of Cocoa and the gang clued Jack in on Wahid's untrustworthiness.

Jack protested. "Look, I know my rights."

"Really, what are they?"

"I have the right to remain silent, I have the right to privacy, and I have the right to not undergo any illegal search or seizure."

"That's impressive, Jack. But you forgot to mention the right to obstruct a murder investigation." Jack swallowed.

"The other problem is that these rights only exist in America or at your Embassy. As it stands, you are in neither place. You may contact them if you like and your device will be returned to you when they make a formal request."

TWENTY SEVEN

Maimonides Synagogue was just wrapping up its weekly Shabbat service. Scribe never imagined so many layers to Cairo. Even in his new digs, he felt like a naked Emperor walking into the Hasidic Jewish quarter. All the men were bearded down to their chests, dressed in black, and wearing oversized shtreimels on their heads. Perhaps a suspended animation laser beam froze everyone's mouths open for blocks. However it happened, the Jewish pedestrians didn't hide their intrigue while watching every move these visitors made.

Scribe flipped his collar. "Guess I showed up to the wrong costume party?"

Mari maintained her pace. "Just keep walking and we'll be fine."

There'd always been a remnant of Jews living in Egypt, even before the death of Solomon and the national split of Israel. Contrary to popular lore, not all Israelites left during the Exodus. Some, like Joseph's sons, stayed because they intermarried, had families, and, eventually, assimilated into Egyptian life. Nevertheless, they remained Jews. When the Muslims came in the seventh century, they coexisted in peace with the Jewish community; even throughout the Crusades…as long as the Jews accepted Islamic rule. There were a few snags here and there, but nothing unmanageable.

"Mari, how many Jews live in Cairo?"

"A few hundred, mostly widows. The native born community is about ninety. In 1948, nearly 80,000 Jews lived in Cairo and Egypt was considered a haven for Jewish culture. This was before the State of Israel. When modern Israel was established, most Jews left Egypt for religious, national, or safety reasons. The ones who stayed have global media protection, but still fear sectarian violence."

Scribe looked back. "Makes sense that they stand on the wall when strangers appear."

"Correct. Although they have had an influx of immigrants, architects, and scholars like your friend, in the past five years."

"How come?"

"ARCE grant money. The American Research Center in Egypt dedicated funds to restore deteriorating historical sites in Egypt's Jewish community."

"That must be why Rock came here."

"Perhaps. Maimonides Synagogue was one of two chosen for restoration."

He knew Maimonides well. Scribe had studied *A Guide for the Perplexed* in graduate school and came away with a synthesis of admiration and confusion. Rabbi Moses Maimonides was a physician, philosopher, and one of the greatest Torah scholars of all time. Maimonides believed in prophets, but not astrology. He believed that God did not get angry, but that it was important for people to think the contrary so they stopped sinning. Scribe never envied the tightrope of being a religious intellectual. Nevertheless, Maimonides had always been a giant in his eyes and Scribe cherished the opportunity to enter the Synagogue named after him.

The gates of the synagogue cast a shadow on a nearby wall. Once one of the most visible signs in the Jewish quarter, rising groundwater damaged the interior of the building and extensive engineering was required to pump it out. Now restored, a sign hung in Hebrew and Arabic welcoming visitors to celebrate Passover within. Mari dropped back and told Scribe he'd better do the talking.

"May I help you?" A tall, broad-shouldered man in his early thirties stood in front of the double glass doors with his hands clasped by his waist. His nametag read 'Ephraim'.

"Yes Ephraim, we're here to see Rabbi Mizrah."

The wary security guard looked at Mari and then back to Scribe. "Is the Rabbi expecting you?"

"No, but he knows a friend of mine: Rabbi Matthew Rockman."

Ephraim's wrinkled forehead suggested that he either didn't know Rockman or didn't know if Scribe was telling the truth. Whichever was the case, he decided to check it out.

"Please be seated. Someone will be with you in a moment."

They sat on a cast iron bench a few steps to the right of the sanctuary. The guard ducked in and spoke to an usher whose head disappeared when the door swung shut. Immediately in front of them stood a portrait of Yacoub Cattaui, the patriarch of a major Egyptian-Jewish family. Resting anterior sat a reader's stand flanked by two ionic pillars and a hovering platform resembling the Ark support in Solomon's Temple. Mari balanced on the edge of the bench, back straight and hands on her knees.

The ushers propped the sanctuary doors open. Elderly Jews filed out as the benediction music played. Appearing pleased to see Scribe and Mari, the worshippers uniformly greeted them with the words "Happy Sabbath"; to which the two responded in kind. The group processed toward a courtyard garden for post-service wine and cheese. Mari's shoulders lowered and she scooted until her back reached the bench railings.

Abruptly, the sanctum doors burst open and a man with thick dark eyebrows and hairy arms came stomping toward the pair, rolling up his sleeves. By the apologetic expression on the face of the usher in tow, Scribe surmised who Mr. Unibrow must be.

"Get the hell out of here on my Sabbath!"

The short, stocky man stood over Scribe with his fists curled. Scribe could feel the panting against his face. Mari turned toward the wall and stormed out the front door like she was arguing with herself, leaving Scribe to face the Rabbi alone. He didn't understand what she was doing, but there was no time to worry about it.

Scribe tried the disarming approach. "I just need to ask about Matthew Rockman. We're friends."

"How dare you come in here during Passover?" The Rabbi's eyes glazed. Scribe imagined smoke billowing from Rabbi Mizrah's nostrils and couldn't help but feel as if he were draped in Jack's favorite color.

Seeing the encounter going nowhere, Scribe decided enough was enough. "How do you reconcile being a man of God with your behavior?"

The Rabbi looked stunned by the challenge. Scribe turned the knife.

"No, how can you have the name of Moses Maimonides on this building but ignore the advice of Proverbs 18:2?"

Blustering, Mizrah peered at Scribe, calculating his next move. His pause told Scribe the message had registered. Maimonides was Jewish clergy but, as a Scholastic philosopher, prized wisdom and reason over blind piety. And Solomon, the wisest of all men had written in Proverbs 18:2 that 'A fool does not delight in understanding, but only in expressing his opinion.' Mizrah looked at the ushers to see if they understood how deeply Scribe's insult had cut. His unibrow gained a fresh crinkle.

"Who let him in here?"

The ushers cringed. The only sound made after the Rabbi spun on his heels and b-lined for the courtyard was the one he bellowed like Ralph Cramdon: "Ephraim!"

Outside, Scribe found Mari on the steps hugging her knees to her chest and wiping single tears as they rolled past her nostrils. He put his feelings of abandonment on hold.

"What's wrong?"

"I knew I shouldn't have gone in?"

Scribe felt guilty for suggesting that they come. "I know. That Rabbi was a primo jerk. But there's no way we could have known that." She gave Scribe a Meg Ryan look. Before she could speak, the gardener tapped her shoulder.

"Mari?"

She froze and slowly peered up, retracing the path of the voice. "Mr. Zogby?" She jumped up and hugged the octogenarian. He twirled her around like a dervish in a trance of joy.

The elderly man spoke in creaky waves. "I thought I'd never see you again. Where have you been? Too long, much too long."

"David, meet Mr. Zogby. He was the only person who was nice to me while I grew up here."

Scribe didn't know what to say without it sounding awkward. But at this point, awkwardness couldn't be helped. "You're Jewish?"

"I grew up Jewish. It was so long ago, I'd almost forgotten how much I hate this place."

Scribe tried to ask the broadest question that came to mind. "What happened?"

She kept her arm around Zogby's waist. He was a slender man of Lebanese descent who'd kept the grounds clean at Maimonides Synagogue for over fifty years. He'd seen a lot of things in that time; some things he talked about, some he didn't. But Mari had been one of the bright spots that helped him endure the invisibility he suffered at work.

"My father loved a Syrian woman and secretly married her without the approval of their parents. They were outcasts in Syria so, after I was born, they settled several kilometers from here in a poor Muslim section of Cairo. He built a small house and we were happy together. My mother kept Islam but agreed to attend Shabbat with us on the weekend. The leaders of the Synagogue would always remind my father that the Torah teaches that Jews are the chosen people and warns against intermingling. They said this meant there were pure races made by God that should be kept separate."

Scribe sputtered. "But that goes against everything we've learned in the last two hundred years."

Mari cleared her throat. "The overseers did not see it that way. Rabbi Mizrah was young then, but ambitious and spiteful. He antagonized our family and encouraged the other children to tease and call me half-breed in that same courtyard." Mari pointed. "When my parents decided to leave the community, I was relieved but knew that they were giving up everything they had for me."

She squeezed Zogby's waist. "I never thought to see you again." The wrinkles in Zogby's smile curved his face into a Sioux medicine man's.

Mari sniffled. "We moved deep into the heart of Cairo, where no Jewish people ever went, and took on my mother's Islam until my parents died."

Scribe's voice inflected. "Mari, I'm so sorry. I could have gone in alone."

"I know, but I didn't want you to. I remember how they can be and I wanted you to have someone there. It's been so long that I don't think anyone recognized me, but his negativity was too much. I had to get out."

"I understand." Scribe sensed…something, then leafed through all that had just happened.

"Mr. Zogby, did you ever meet Rabbi Matthew Rockman. He's an American, about this tall, and always has a shoulder bag like mine?" Scribe presented the strap of his laptop.

Zogby rested his free arm on the rail. "As a matter of fact, I did. He came here last July to work with the ARCE project and taught a few Torah classes in his spare time. I could tell Rabbi Mizrah disapproved because Rabbi Rockman was friendly and the people liked him. The next month he began teaching a Christianity class at the American University on Friday evenings and Mizrah forbid it. Since that day, he has not been back."

Scribe pressed. "How do you know all of this?"

"He told me. I was the only one around here who would talk to Rabbi Rockman after Mizrah admonished the others against keeping company with him. Also, I have no problem talking about Jesus." A familiar twinkle brightened Zogby's pupils.

Scribe couldn't believe it. All he could think of were Gloria's words, "People get messages everyday and just shrug them off as coincidence."

Mari's eyes turned colors again. "What is it?"

"I'll tell you later. But maybe somebody at the University has an idea of what Rock was working on."

"Let's find out." She hugged Zogby goodbye and made another promise to visit next week. As she did, a European motorcyclist turned a slow corner too sharply and had to lay his bike down. The German-built moped skidded one way while his torso and hands skid another. He'd make it through without any major medical intervention, but needed to be patched up.

Scribe and Zogby pulled the man out of the street and Mari grabbed the moped. He was groggy but could walk, barely. Watching, Mari noticed Rabbi Mizrah and Ephraim standing at the glass door. *How long have they been there?*, she wondered.

Mizrah came out with both hands in front, palms out. "Don't bring him up here bleeding on my Shabbat." Scribe was incredulous. Zogby had the stoic face of a man in Angola prison denied parole for the third time.

Scribe sniped, "Even I get the point about doing good on the Sabbath", alluding to Jesus scolding the Pharisees and healing the man with the withered hand.

Zogby spoke in a low tone, locking eyes with Mizrah. "You two go ahead. I'll take care of him."

Mizrah eyeballed Mari talking on her phone, gritted his teeth at Zogby, then back to Mari. *Where do I know you from?*, he pondered.

Scribed helped lay Evel Kneivel onto the grass and jogged to catch up with her. The Rabbi pulled Ephraim's hand off the door bar and wrenched him away from the twilight.

"Let the Gentile attend to his own."

TWENTY EIGHT

When Jack protested the confiscation of his Blackberry, that was all Cocoa needed to break away from Rick and Terry.

"I know you dirty cops aren't trying to steal this man's phone."

Wahid intentionally breathed through his nostrils. "Ma'am, we believe the contents of this device could aid in our investigation. Legally we can sequester it."

"Well everything legal ain't right. I know that. Is it right for women to walk around with their eyeballs covered in the summer while men wear short-sleeve shirts and sip iced tea?"

The female servers in the room hazarded a glance, shocked but eager to hear the Inspector's response.

"This is a cultural occurrence. It is our way."

Cocoa's hand rested on her shapely hips. "Humph. Your *way* is messed up. What if it were you suffocating under those blankets? Then you wouldn't be so quick to sweep that heatstroke under the rug."

Score one for Westerville. The female servers hid their giggles.

Wahid faced Jack. "Sir, if you do not surrender the device I will be forced to secure it at the precinct after detaining you."

Cocoa stepped back into his field of vision. "So you're going to arrest Jack over his phone? Whatever. You try it and see what happens."

Jack saw it coming but all he could do was watch. He remembered that time they debated in Maryland and one of the opponents snickered while Cocoa was speaking. She resumed and everything was fine. But when the opponent mumbled that she sounded like Rosie Perez, she politely scooted her chair back, mermaided to his end of the table, and whacked him so hard with her microphone that the sound guys snatched off their headsets.

"I got your Rosie Perez", she'd said as he recoiled. "It looks like white men can jump after all."

The whole team, even Scribe, was so stunned afterwards that they didn't realize Cocoa resumed talking as if nothing ever happened. The debater was too embarrassed to press charges and the coaches agreed to call the match a tie. They laughed about Mr. Maryland falling out of his chair all the way home.

She had that same mischievous glint in her eyes, that pre-destruction look of Dennis the Menace. Jack stepped up and offered the phone.

"Here you go man. We don't want any problems."

Cocoa huffed and squinted. "I know you're not gonna let him take your phone?"

"To keep you out jail? Yes."

Cocoa's cheekbones rose. However, her 'That's so sweet' face to Jack morphed into a 'You'll never take me alive' lip curl when she turned back to Wahid.

Cocoa growled. "I'm not going to jail." Her dramatic pause prefaced her fists clenching. She resumed. "He knows if he takes me to jail, he's got to take us all..." Cocoa scanned the room before ending, "...because that's how we roll." Rick and Terry vigorously shook their heads, pleading with Wahid.

"Have it your way, madam. Detectives?"

Wahid motioned for the uniformed officers to take them all into custody. Rick and Terry kicked at figurative pebbles before following the lead of the detective toward the elevator. Jack imagined Cocoa anchoring her feet across the doorframe like Ma Barker, refusing to be dragged out. To the astonishment of the entire room, she calmly held her chin up, placed her hands by her sides with fingertips pointing outward, and sauntered across the floor like Cleopatra.

Jack's heart thumped palpably.

"No one is going to jail", a woman's voice said matter-of-factly.

Everyone stopped and wafted toward the sound with inquiring minds.

"Who are you?" Wahid challenged more to establish his authority than to gather information.

With a rehearsed flair, the diminutive woman stood her ground, smiled slightly, and straightened her suit jacket, "I'm Dr. Delores Chamberlain, President of Westerville University."

Back at the precinct Wahid licked his wounds, thankful that he got out of the room with the phone and his career in tact. Like the rest of the world, political power in Cairo heavily depended on economic currents. The Student-Exchange Program brought much needed visibility to Cairo's modernity and intellectual pursuits, which translated to grant money currently supplementing dwindling tourism dollars.

When Chamberlain revealed that she knew Chief Habash personally and had dined with him after last year's concert, Wahid treaded lightly. Luckily, she'd instructed Jack to hand over his phone and put Cocoa in check with the evil eye, avoiding further incident. But the victory was short-lived. By the time he returned to his desk Habash was waiting for him, fuming.

"I ask you to keep this quiet and you're about to arrest four American students?"

Wahid stood there hoping the question was rhetorical. The flaring of Habash's nostrils indicated after a few seconds that it wasn't.

"Sir, those students were obstructing the investigation."

"Inspector, I don't care if they were pee peeing on the Pyramids. They're kids. You know kids go pee pee, don't you?"

Wahid was not amused, but kept a straight face.

Habash switched gears. "So what have you got?"

"The computer techs retrieved the email the 'kid' sent to our prime suspect. It was a translation of the attachment he deleted from Rockman's original communication."

"And?"

"It's a series of Bible verses surrounding the resurrection of Jesus."

"That's it?"

"So far. Our guys are still working on making sense of it."

"Well make sense of this: If you don't bring this guy in, your career is over. I knew I should have promoted your girlfriend instead of you. Now she's helping the guy you can't seem to catch to save your life."

Wahid's temperature rose.

The officer on phone duty handed Habash a note. "You'd better pray I don't get fired during this call or you can pack your desk up, drink blood, and eat crackers with your brothers."

He knew. How long?

Habash snarled. "That's right, I know your little secret. And I have no intention of letting you steal my job. As of now, you still work for me. Enough of this Bible verse nonsense. Do some real police work and bring Scribe in." Habash began to stomp away then turned back. "Forget the Rabbi. I want the man who killed Saba, dead or alive, tonight!"

TWENTY NINE

The taxi driver gladly took the twenty dollar bill Scribe handed him. It was the smallest bill Scribe had. The fare had only been two dollars but, of course, the driver didn't have any change. Scribe chalked it up to money that would come back to him in his next lifetime as a used car dealer. Mari had already started up the massive walkway before he ran to catch up.

The American University in Cairo was considered the premier English-language institution in the Arab world. The dignitaries attending the inauguration of AUC's new Cairo location had included the First Lady of Egypt and other foreign ambassadors. Even the President of the United States sent his congratulations on opening day of the state-of-the-art, $400 million complex spanning 260 acres. The brochure tacked to the foyer bulletin board broadcasted these facts and further declared that the campus 'weaves together traditional Egyptian architecture with urban modernity and places a distinct emphasis on environmental sustainability.'

Some of this was true. The physical plant radiated magnificence, giving the feel of a luxurious vacation spot rather than sterile laboratories, classrooms, and desks. There were public spaces constructed to encourage group dialogue beneath archways fit for the Taj Mahal. Niches for theater and the arts were carved alongside those for science and engineering. Green power fueled the learning community, making it an oasis for great possibilities. Taking in the physical plant through wide lenses, Scribe admitted that AUC was enviable by any standards anywhere on the planet. Yet he couldn't ignore the irony that the biotechnology and environmental conscientiousness visibly halted at the campus border.

"Unless they have giant smog sucking machines that rise from the rooftops at night, so much for sustaining the environment. They could've saved a ton of money by giving everyone a brand new muffler or outlawing Camel cigarettes."

Mari liked Scribe's sense of humor. He was sharp and witty in the way her father had been. Her childhood was bearable in part because of her father's jovial cynicism. She reminisced while scanning Rockman's office door. "The schedule says Room 245. It's almost 8:30 and the class started at 7 pm."

There was no Department of Religion at AUC. In a country where Islam was publicly tied to citizenship, it wouldn't do to have professors teaching things that disrupted the fabric of society. Intellectual freedom and curiosity were fine in the sciences, but tenure could not save a dissenting Academic in the Humanities from the Board of Supervisors or an angry mob. Nevertheless, informing students about the differences between Islam and other faiths was deemed acceptable. Therefore Rockman had been invited by the History Department to teach two courses for their newly established minor in Comparative Religion.

"He probably has a Teaching Assistant for times when he's late. Hopefully the class is still here." Scribe hadn't yet been able to speak about Rockman in the past tense.

A quick peek into Room 245 yielded no notes on the blackboard and no TA stationed to lead the absent class. Scribe and Mari strode toward the lectern as if they hoped someone would gradually appear as they moved in closer. They found the room completely empty. No books, no notes, not even a used nub of chalk.

The classroom reminded Scribe of his students. "Let's see if Jack made any progress."

Wireless technology was a wonderful thing. Scribe always carried his plug-in modem, but he didn't need it here. The entire campus was a Wi-Fi hotspot and, after connecting with the AUC server, Scribe was sailing the web in no time.

Two junk emails from people guaranteeing 25% return on investment despite the global recession and one promising male enhancement hovered above the subject line: "FUZZ HERE".

There was no attachment, just text. Jack had inserted a rough translation of each line underneath the original. The only other comments from Jack were "koine greek bible verses. gotta go before pretty boy makes his move"

Typical 20 year old male: Girls and Greek. Scribe chuckled aloud at his own mental wordplay.

"What is it?" Mari rotated the device so she had a better view.

"Jack cracked the attachment."

"What does it say?"

Scrolling, Scribe answered. "It seems to be a collection of New Testament Bible verses taken from the four Gospels."

Mari gave a puzzled look.

"Some of them are repetitive but they appear to concern the last week of Jesus' life."

They stared in different directions until Mari broke the silence.

"Do you think that someone had your friend murdered because of his interest in Jesus? It may seem petty in America, but people here take religious lines very seriously. Some smaller communities still stone for blasphemy. It's illegal, but no one confesses and authorities turn a blind eye."

"It's possible. But why now? Rock was as out of the closet about his love affair with Jesus as you could get. If someone wanted to take him out for that, why wait until now?"

"Maybe they wanted to make a statement. It *is* Passion week, which is also Passover week for Jews. Killing him now sends a clear message about betrayal or, at least, keeping the religious lines uncrossed."

The cop in Mari was showing itself. From the treatment they'd received at the synagogue, it wasn't hard to believe Mizrah had the disposition to order a hit on Rockman. He'd practically watched a man suffer a fatal motorcycle crash and hadn't lifted a finger to help. It wasn't a far stretch for Scribe to imagine Mizrah not flinching at ordering a wayward Rabbi eliminated. If he considered Rockman a rival, it would have been even easier. Still it didn't sit well with Scribe.

"I see that, Mari. But what about the dagger with the 'praise Allah' writing?"

"Planted."

Scribe swung his knees around touching hers. "What's your theory?"

She took a deep breath and began. "I know this is a Muslim country, but most of us do not run around with pictures of Allah on our shirts or our backpacks. This tells me that a killer choosing a dagger with the most widespread phrase in Islam written on the handle is either a member of an extremist group or employed it to implicate a Muslim, which effectively eliminates all suspects."

Scribe considered her theory, nodding. Masters in Criminology or not, she thought outside the box. He liked that. The intrigue of it all tugged at him.

"Okay. Let's say I go along with the Muslim being framed idea." He'd been trapped inside so many hypotheticals in the last two days, Scribe felt like he was back in Torts class during his only year of Law School. "It's no secret that you don't care for Rabbi Mizrah. I'm worried that your hypo points to him mainly because he's won the 'butthole-of-the-year award' ever since you were a girl."

Mari pushed her chair back, stung. "Are you saying that I am trying to make Mizrah sound guilty?" Mari waited intensely.

"Not trying, just...predisposed. Everybody does that sometimes, right?" His diving save hadn't worked. Flaring nostrils on woman: bad.

Mari rejoined. "I am not saying that Mizrah killed Rockman. I am suggesting the plausibility of building a model around the killer as a non-Muslim, given the backlash Rockman received from members of the Jewish community." By 'community' she meant Mizrah, but she didn't say his name. Instead, she tilted her head and feigned a smile.

Faintly, they heard sobs coming from the doorway. A young woman, petite, twentyish and slender with frizzy brown hair pulled back into a ponytail mostly overlain with a headscarf braced herself on the left side of the doorframe. She had strong cheekbones and a smooth complexion. The rest of her face was hidden behind long, bony fingers that covered her eyes and made her lips seem unnaturally thin.

Mari ran to steady the young woman and helped her to an available seat. After a minute of non-stop tears and Mari repeating, "It's okay. What's wrong?", the woman took her hands from her face and blew until she cleared both nasal passages.

"Thank you for the tissue."

"Of course", Scribe responded tenderly. "Tell us what's the matter."

"I am Adeena, Professor Rockman's Teaching Assistant for the Christology class. I am a graduate student in the History Department and have been privileged to work with him for the past two semesters. I cannot believe he is gone." She started crying again and Scribe handed her more Kleenex.

"What is this 'Christology'?", Mari puzzled.

Scribe answered. "Christology concerns the deity of Christ. New Testament accounts of Jesus range from 'son of man' to 'son of God' to 'God', depending on who was writing and who was being written to. Rock liked to look at the different way each of the four biblical Gospels talked about Jesus. I can hear him saying now:

"Matthew was writing to Jews, so none of that son of God stuff for him. For that guy, Jesus was 'son of man' all the way. But John was writing to Greeks, so he uses philosophy and concepts like 'logos' to say that Jesus was both fully divine and fully human. Different audience, different version of Jesus."

Seeing Adeena and talking about Rockman made Scribe miss him again. As far as he could tell, she was the only other person wishing that this were all a bad dream. That bond made him want to share the truth with her. "Adeena, he was killed on Wednesday evening in Old Cairo."

Adeena had a quiet panic in her eyes. "But why?", she whispered in pain. A tear fell as her face reddened. "What was he doing there?"

"We don't know. That's what we're trying to figure out."

Placing his hands on his chest, Scribe spoke the way Gloria had spoken to him. "Adeena, I'm David Scribe and this is my friend, Mari."

Her features softened. "Dr. Scribe, he mentioned you often. He said you were his best friend and that he missed talking to you."

"Rock said that?" Scribe was touched. He thought of Rockman as his best friend too, but didn't know the feeling was mutual.

"Yes, on a number of occasions. He said he couldn't break his routine before the time. However he promised that, when it was done, he would tell me all about his work and contact you.

Scribe's mind raced. She might actually be able to fill in some missing pieces. "When is the last time you saw Rock, I mean, Professor Rockman?"

"Wednesday morning. We always had breakfast on Wednesday morning to go over the lecture and any questions I might have about the material. Every class period, he would let me lead a portion of the discussion for practice and experience. But this week was our last class meeting. The class expected to see him before I gave the final examination tonight, but he never came."

Breakfast every week? That's more time than we used to spend together, Scribe calculated.

Adeena frowned. "I feel ashamed for being upset with him. He said he had something special for me that he would give me after class. That's why I was waiting across the hall. We sometimes use that room because the desks are bigger and there is never any chalk in this one."

"So you knew Rock pretty well?"

"Yes, I did."

Mari leaned in, signaling that she wanted to ask the next question. "Adeena, were you two involved romantically?" She said the last two words gingerly.

"Yes and no. I knew as a Rabbi and a faculty member, it was forbidden for us to cross certain boundaries. Much of our interaction was long talks and hand holding. Goodbye kisses twice. But Rocky said that after this semester, he would no longer be on staff and we would be free to explore our relationship."

"Rocky?" Scribe and Mari repeated in unison. Scribe's brow furrowed.

Mari continued. "Where did you meet for breakfast?"

"At his apartment. The University gave him campus housing but it was too public for him. He would use it in the daytime, yet slept and worked in the apartment at night. It is five minutes from here in Zamalek Residence. He cooked the best scrambled eggs and kosher meals."

Mari didn't look at Scribe. Aside from the identification card Adeena clipped to her lanyard, she wore an electric blue blouse with white piping around the collar, denim culottes, and white canvas Keds with no socks. Her outfit was thoroughly Western and cosmopolitan; however, the hand-crafted brass bracelet displaying the star and crescent moon on her wrist re-opened the list of suspects again.

Mari took her hand. "Adeena, do you have an old boyfriend or know of anyone else that might have noticed how close you were to Dr. Rockman?"

"I do not think so. We never had public affection and I always used the back entrance to the apartment." She pulled an object from her front pocket.

Scribe ogled. "You have a key?"

"Oh, yes. Rocky gave it to me to unlock the rear entrance gate so I could come and go undetected."

Scribe saw the numbers 1240 as he held it up to the light. "A secret apartment? Rocky, you little devil." He wiggled his eyebrows like Groucho Marx.

Adeena gave a melancholy smile. "He said he picked it because of Matthew 12:40. He was so fascinated by the resurrection. One of the things I love about him is that he is free being himself."

As if realizing Rockman was dead for the first time, Adeena again sobbed through her hands. Sniffling, she managed the breathless words, "I have to go to the bathroom", let out an agonized moan, and stumbled down the hallway.

Mari grimaced. "For all we know, she could have been hoping for an engagement ring."

"Yeah, poor kid."

Scribe stared at the tile before performing an internet search.

"You won't believe it. The first verse is Matthew 12:40."

Mari read the computer screen:

Matthew 12:40: 'For as Jonah was three days and three nights in the whale's belly; so shall the Son of man be three days and three nights in the heart of the earth.'

She sighed. "Jesus verses?"

"Looks like it. I think Jesus is talking about how long he's going to be buried after he dies. The comparison is with Jonah." Scribe grinned.

Mari picked up on his shift. "What is it?"

"Nothing really. It's just that you always hear people ragging on how the Bible says that Jonah was swallowed by a big fish, not a whale. I guess Jesus was part human after all because he obviously got the story wrong, too."

"What do you think your friend meant, David?"

"I don't know. Ordinarily I'd think he meant to show me that 'whale' part for a good laugh. But with all that's happened, I'd have to look at the other verses to get a better idea."

Scribe's temples constricted, then he focused on the wall to the left of Mari's ear. "Did you hear something?"

"No. Did you?"

"Maybe." Scribe checked his watch. "Hey, where's Adeena? She should've been back by now."

Mari's phone beeped. "I'll go check on her. Hello...", she said walking out of the room.

In addition to Adeena, Scribe wondered about the phone calls Mari received and conveniently answered when he wasn't within earshot. She'd just hung up as he came toward her outside the synagogue, but in all the excitement, he let it go. This time he was going to ask. She said she had been a cop and, for all he knew, she still was; undercover and assigned to report his whereabouts to Wahid.

Scribe packed his laptop, hung the pouch across his body, and turned left into the hallway. Before registering the scenario, his pulse raced wildly and his nerves tingled like the volume of everything around him had been amplified. Yet the only sound he actually heard were his own mental screams as he sprinted toward the end of the corridor. In a pregnant, surreal moment he saw a pair of canvas Keds jutting out of the women's bathroom toes up; and what looked like Lou Ferrigno choking a small child with long black hair from behind. The hooded Sasquatch silently squeezed the life out its victim like a boa constrictor.

Kicking frantically, Mari wedged her feet against the wall and pushed off like her swim team days at King Abdullah Academy. The creature stepped back to keep its balance when...*Crack!*

The monster released its grip and fell hard, twitching and holding the side of his skull with both hands.

It all happened so fast. Without thinking, Scribe ran blind and barehanded to save the dying woman who had been his guide since this morning. When he got within ten steps of them, the thing choking Mari teetered backwards. The juggling pouch slapping his ribcage communicated its desire. Smoothly, Scribe lifted the strap over his head, pirouetted like an Alvin Ailey dancer, and delivered a Hank Aaron swing that would have broken all records for the longest homerun.

His high school teammates used to call him professor, but everyone thought he'd end up playing major league ball. So did he. That is, until he started having trouble with his rotator cuff. Scribe could still hit the ball a mile, but nobody wanted to draft him just to hit. A baseball player that can't throw is like a dog that can't bite. You don't pay five million dollars a year for a toothless dog with a scary bark. He'd tried out a few times, but there were lots of guys that could do both. So no callbacks. Being a professor just kind of 'happened'. Maybe it was meant to be. Good thing he still swung for the fence.

Scribe scooped Mari up, intending to carry her to the stairwell, but she startled him by jumping out of his arms, swinging and gasping for air until she got it. Sucking in lungfuls, she braced herself on the corner wall where the canvas Keds propped open the lavatory door. Adeena's lips and hands had already begun to blue and her eyes were horribly bulged. There were deep impressions on her esophagus and her neck appeared grotesquely bowed against the cream colored tile on the bathroom floor. Her distraught state made her an easy target, still clutching Kleenex in her left hand. 'Poor kid' didn't begin to describe Adeena's misfortune.

"Mari, are you alright?"

Panting, she gave him a series of fast nods but stopped abruptly. She pushed Scribe aside and charged behind him screaming. The cloaked killer had rolled to his knees and was trying to pull himself up using the wall. Perhaps it was Police Academy judo training or primordial rage, but Mari sliced through the air landing such a fierce heel kick to the Keeper's jaw that she refreshed his open cranium wound. This time he slumped to the polished surface without a sound.

Mari scrambled to her feet and rejoined Scribe. "I'm fine now."

"Is there something I need to know? Something you're not telling me?" Scribe's childhood urban accent emerged.

"What?" Mari could see Scribe's chest rising and falling. She knew from experience that his adrenaline was high and they both could be in a mild state of shock. Most of all she knew they needed to move.

Questions ricocheted in Scribe's head like well hit pinballs. Mari could read his mind but thought better of starting a conversation right then.

Interlocking their fingers, she tugged. "Let's get out of here first."

Any hesitation on Scribe's part was massaged by Mari's gesture and eliminated by the stirring of Mr. Ferrigno. Neither of them saw if he revived or still lay moaning on the floor. Mari loosed Scribe's hand and they hit the stairwell like Jesse Owens chasing Jackie Joyner Kersey for Olympic gold.

The security guard had his legs elevated, thumbing through the 'Sexiest-Covers' edition of Egyptian Lifestyle Magazine. He felt the wind of bodies in motion whiz past, but with a campus full of 18-25 year olds, that happened ten times a day, everyday. Not until he heard a shrill scream come from the second floor did he consider the couple that flew out the entrance. By the time he picked up his walkie-talkie and looked, Scribe and Mari had left the Taj Mahal arches and were galloping through the expanse of fountains dividing the walkway.

THIRTY

When **Wahid** pulled into AUC's parking lot, he marveled that so many reporters were on the scene and still arriving. Wahid flashed his badge to the campus rent-a-cops and crossed over the yellow crime scene tape. Students surrounded the building with candles, hearing that one of their own had been murdered but not knowing who. Some cried, some just stared with mouths agape, feeling that the innocence of their Utopia had been forever compromised.

"Who's in charge here?" Wahid scanned the uniformed personnel like the Terminator.

"I am." A fiftyish man with oversized hands and forearms that put Popeye to shame stepped forward. "Azreel Jibran, Head of Campus Police."

The two men shook.

"Inspector Wahid, CPD. What do we have here?"

"AUC student, Adeena Karos, found strangled by Sondia Aleem, editor of the campus newspaper."

Jibran pointed to the window where a heavyset teenager peered down at the flashing lights surrounded by the growing hoards of people.

"Ms. Aleem? Salaama."

"Salaama brother." Wahid usually didn't correct anyone when they assumed he was Muslim. Neither did he here."

After introducing himself, he asked her to recount the sequence of events for the third time that evening.

"...Did you see anyone else when you exited the elevator?"

"No one, just Adeena."

"You know her?"

"Yes. She was the Teaching Assistant for Christology with Professor Rockman. I'm..."

Wahid blanked out after the word. His mind skipped like a CD with a deep scratch at the mention of Rockman. The events of the last 48 hours flooded into the present. *Rockman, Saba, now this girl?* He saw the black bag zipped halfway, exposing Adeena's head and torso. The brutality of extinguishing a life so young made Wahid's eyes mist.

"So this girl was Rabbi Matthew Rockman's assistant?"

"Yes. We had our final exam this evening and I returned to see if she could give me an idea of what my grade would be. I was the last one to finish and had been gone about thirty minutes."

"Were they...you know?" He gestured a kissing face.

"What do you mean, brother? Oh no, Allah." She placed her hand over her chest and fluttered her eyelashes. "I know nothing of this."

Wahid pretended to scratch her response down in his pad before resuming. "Did you call anyone after the police?"

"Not that I can remember. But I am in charge of the *Caravan* and AUC students deserve to know from their campus newspaper the truth of what happened here."

Wahid looked out the window again and considered the words of his witness. Before he could conclude the interview, his cell phone rang. He looked up at Sondia. "Excuse me, I need to take this call. Hello…"

"Update?" This was Habash's one word way of saying, 'Tell me you have the killer in custody or tell me when your resignation will be on my desk.'

"Sorry Chief, more problems."

"What problems?"

"Got called to a murder on the AUC campus. Turned out to be Rockman's female Teaching Assistant."

"His what?" Habash snorted. "Was their relationship strictly professional?"

"As far as I'm told, there was nothing between them. But if there was, we can use the jealous lover angle with the media to buy more time."

"You don't have any more time. I want someone in jail for these murders tonight or I want your resignation in the morning. Do you understand that?"

"I understand."

"Good. Now tell me what the evidence suggests?"

"I haven't studied it yet, but there doesn't seem like much. Hold on, Chief…" Wahid needed a break before he said something to Habash that would make a resignation unnecessary. He muffled the receiver and turned to Sondia.

"Did you touch anything when you found her?"

"No. I screamed and the security guard came up as I was calling the police. I handed him the phone and overheard him say he saw a man and a woman running across the courtyard right before he came upstairs."

"Did he say what they looked like?"

"He said it was dark and he didn't get a good look at them. All he could see was the woman's hair blowing and the man's shoulder bag flopping against his side."

Wahid jammed the phone back to his ear and took off in search of the security guard.

THIRTY ONE

Mari and Scribe tiptoed into the sparsely furnished apartment. It was neat but thinly appointed with an aging, rust-hued sofa, twin bed, analog TV, and a flimsy computer desk. A card table rounded out the ensemble accented by two folding chairs, a doily tablecloth, and a flute vase housing pink carnations.

Closing the blinds, he faced Mari. "Who is this clown and why is he trying to kill us?"

Mari rested her fingertips on her forehead. "I couldn't see his face, except for his beard."

Scribe removed his bag. "I hope this thing still works. I don't think using it as a bola is covered under the warranty."

Mari's voice softened. "Thank you, again. That is twice today you saved me."

"I know. Next time I'm charging." They both plopped onto the sofa in exhaustion.

Mari turned, pinning her knee against the back cushion. "It seems that Adeena's information was reliable."

"Too reliable. Looks like that maniac thought so, too. Do you think he knows about this place?"

Mari shook her head. "If he did, it would probably have been invaded or on fire by now."

"I guess you're right. Adeena wouldn't have made it this long either, if he knew the extent of her and Rock's relationship."

Scribe flurried his hands like Vanna White. The elephants in the room were the myriad of framed pictures adorning the walls. Adeena eating breakfast. Adeena on the sofa. Adeena laughing. Adeena hiding her face. Adeena, Adeena, Adeena. Between the rabbit ears of the dated Samsung television stood a picture of Adeena and Rock smiling, faces too big as if they took the picture themselves.

"It seems that your friend found more in Egypt than some Bible verses." Her comment returned Scribe's mind to the laptop.

Scribe unzipped his bag and pulled out the silver rectangle in tact. It was dented from the cranial impact with Bigfoot but had seen worse days. Unfortunately, snapped off in one of the ports was the wireless modem connector. "When it rains, it pours."

"David, there's a computer in the corner."

Scribe inspected the terminal. "No phone line, though. It's only hooked up to a printer."

"So what do we do? You need the internet to see your email, right?"

"Yeah, but I had a feeling that I should save Jack's file on my desktop before I came into the hallway. I really can't explain why I did. The only thing that comes to mind is that I felt somehow compelled."

Waiting for the processor to boot up, Scribe risked a question. "Mari, remember when we were at St. George's running down the steps?"

She nodded.

"Did you hear somebody call my name?"

"No. I didn't hear anything except Saba hit the ground. Did you?"

"It was strange. I heard someone shout 'Dave' and, if I didn't know better, I could've sworn it was Rock."

Mari remained blank. Scribe continued.

"I mean nobody around there knew me and certainly no one would've called me 'Dave'. But Rock used to call me that all the time."

"I'm sorry, I did not hear it. But good for us you did. This brings back the words of your sensitive."

"It does. But I'm not sure I want to hear voices that other people don't. Seems like the first step to the crazy house."

Mari frowned. Scribe repeated a circular motion near his temple with his index finger. She smiled in recognition.

"Insane? I see. Perhaps in the West. But people of faith all over the world have spoken of hearing voices and having conversations with the dead. In Judaism, King Saul spoke with the recently deceased Samuel and Jesus is reported as speaking with Moses and Elijah on a mountaintop. The last two were long dead."

Scribe visualized the references and pointed at Mari like she'd thrown him an alley-oop. "So I'm either a lunatic or a prophet?"

"In some cultures, they are one and the same." She pointed back with droopy eyes.

Scribe caught the pass. "Get some sleep. I'm going to search Rock's computer to see what's there. I doubt that I'll find anything, though. Rock was paranoid about people stealing his work so he always carried it with him. He only did mundane things on his home PC and, judging from the absence of a phone line in here, he may have used this one even less."

After five minutes, Mari was horizontal on the sofa. Scribe's preliminary search of the computer yielded a game of Mine Sweep, Solitaire, and a music player with Soft Rock and 80's hits. As much as Scribe loved Air Supply and Michael McDonald, he had no time to stroll down memory lane. The last thing he found within the media storage made him glance with delight at Mari's outstretched form. It was an electronic version of the Bible.

"Daddy, can I play the Gameboy when we get home?"

"Yes, baby. But turn around and let Daddy finish typing. We'll be home in a minute." Scribe massaged the left shoulder of the driver. "Honey you okay up there?"

"Uh huh. Wednesdays are just so long with Bible study. It's all we can do to get home, eat, and get in the bed before the next day begins."

"Lena, I already told you we can start our own chain of churches. Our slogan will be 'Beside Baptist: One Near You."

Lena and Amy always giggled when Scribe told that one. They had finally made it through the hard days of graduate school, diapers, and Similac. If that wasn't enough, they'd done what most academic couples never could. They'd landed solid teaching positions in the same city. In six months, she'd be at Bernaux, an elite Women's College and he'd worked out a deal with Westerville that gave him a year's credit toward tenure if he could finish his first book before he arrived. Like the name of the scholarship that paid his way through school, 'Life Gets Better'... at least for a while.

An evasive swerve. Garbled cries. Two cars. Wrong way. Glass breaking. Wet wind. Midair. Landed hard. Disoriented. Blue lights. Running. Strapped in. Both gone. Laptop on asphalt. Blackout.

Scribe awakened sweaty, yanking at the headboard of Rockman's undersized bed. The dreams had decreased over time and he hadn't had one in a while but, when he did, they were always intense. In cobra position, he tasted the fresh flavor of pillowcase and massaged an aching sensation in his back from sleeping on his stomach. The moonrays were adamant yet soft, filing into the cubicle that doubled for Rockman's bedroom. Even after the stretch, Scribe still felt like the Lilliputians had tied him down and run off to fetch more rope. Turning, soreness rolled into every cranny of his muscles; especially the leg that had hovered over the floor for the last hour.

On the side of the bed, head in hands, Scribe heard muffled voices in the outer room. Then...*Smash!* The sound of breaking glass and furniture overturning filled the air. Without shoes, Scribe rushed out to find President Chamberlain swinging a folding chair at the wall photos like the last of the Mohicans. Mari cringed near the door trying to talk her down, but not getting through. After she'd cracked every frame, Chamberlain tossed the chair on the floor and slinked down the wall, weeping.

Scribe rushed through the bedroom door, stopping short of the shards of broken glass littering the floor. "What's going on out here?" He looked at Mari, cutting his eyes to Chamberlain asking a question within a question.

"I...she..." Mari paused and started again. "We were talking and things got a little heated."

"Heated? About what?" Scribe squinted. "Mari, can you tell me something that makes some sense?" He cut his eyes back and forth between them before resting on Chamberlain. "Dr. Chamberlain, what are you doing here?"

Mari looked to the wall. "Dr. Chamberlain, may I?" Chamberlain kept her head down but nodded and waived her hand in permission.

"David. I'm sorry I did not tell you sooner, I was sworn to secrecy."

Scribe rested a hand on the sofa. "What secrecy?"

"Remember when I told you I was a police detective and now I write plays?"

Scribe thought to himself, *And so it begins...* but he simply answered, "Um hmm."

"Indeed, all of this is true. But I neglected to mention that I sometimes work as a private detective."

His breathing quickened and his teeth clenched. "Go on."

"About two months ago I was hired to follow your friend around to see how he spent his days and what kind of things he was doing. I knew he taught at AUC so I watched him from time to time walking across campus or in the dining commons. I made weekly email reports and received electronic payments after each one. One day, I saw your friend with a young woman and they had a 'more than friends' look as they sat talking in the library."

"Adeena?"

"Yes. I did not think much of it and noted it in my report. I received the weekly payment along with the reply that my services would no longer be needed. That was six weeks ago and I haven't seen him since."

Scribe stood with his gaze locked. "Mari, do you know who killed Rock?"

"No." Her tone was soft but her eyes held the gaze.

Scribe swallowed. "Okay, but who was this employer that had you tailing Rock and what is the President of Westerville University doing in this apartment right now?"

"At first I did not know. Then I received a text message telling me that the client would arrive in Cairo today and requested to be secured from the airport after you."

"After me? Do I know...?" Scribe stopped short as if all his questions were answered when a sobering Chamberlain stood to her feet, wiped her eyes, smoothed the ripples in her St. John suit, and spoke.

"Yes, I had him followed. I waited six months for him to call and I couldn't take it any longer. I had to know."

Religion professors don't bring in grant money, so what could she possibly want with Rock? "You had to know what?" Scribe rattled his head and puckered his eyes. "Let me get this straight. You knew where he was all this time?"

Chamberlain stepped closer. "I knew where he was, but what good is that when I couldn't see him?"

Her inflection made Scribe's lips part but nothing came out.

She filled the silence. "When Matthew came to my office for his annual review, he told me he wanted to take a leave of absence to do some research in Egypt. When I asked him the nature of the research he wouldn't say. I pleaded with him not to go, but he wouldn't listen. I was furious when we parted and I yelled. I yelled and he didn't say a word when he left. That was the last time I ever saw him."

"The way you two argued at faculty retreats, I didn't know you cared so much." *I didn't know you cared at all*, he mentally mouthed while keeping the same expression.

Chamberlain's eyes quivered.

Mari broke her vow. "David, she needed to tell him something." Mari moved across the room and pulled Chamberlain's head against her chest. "I'm sorry Delores."

"It's okay. I appreciate what you've done." Chamberlain daubed at her tear ducts with the tissue Mari gave her.

"What did she need to tell him that was so important? Since

you were playing Inspector Gadget, you could've easily delivered the message."

"Not true. That would have blown my cover and, besides, it was not that kind of message."

Scribe was in locomotive mode and not open to slowing just yet. "Well you could've told me that's who you've been talking to all day. I didn't know what to think."

"I apologize. I had to maintain Delores' confidence. She was in no condition to endure any more pain. With our situation, I could not pick her up from the airport so I made alternate arrangements and answered any questions I could about the death of your friend."

Chamberlain slipped between them and sat down on the sofa.

Scribe put his hands on his hips. "So she knows everything?"

"She told me Rabbi Rockman was dead before you arrived. I was rehired before you deplaned to simply keep her informed on the investigation."

"So you did know?" Scribe backed away.

"I did not know he was your friend or that you even knew him. When you told me in the lobby, my reaction was genuine concern for you."

Scribe wanted to believe her, but he felt like he'd been suckered ever since he landed. Nothing made sense and his temperature rose again. "I still don't know what she's doing here."

Before Mari could answer, Scribe fired questions like a Gatling gun. "How do I know you've been telling the truth? How do I know you're not just playing me now, holding back information like you've done since I met you? How do I know you're not working with Wahid to pin all this on me?" Mari backed up with every question and Scribe kept pace. "And how do I know you didn't kill Rock or that she didn't order his death?" He thumbed over his shoulder without looking back.

A shrieking voice came from behind him. "Because I was in love with him, that's why, and I would never have hurt him!" Scribe twisted like a Poltergeist had control of his neck.

THIRTY TWO

Jack and Cocoa shuffled back to their apartment building downloading the day's events. Cocoa was a mile a minute and Jack barely noticed because adrenaline from his near arrest was still coursing through his veins. His silence, while normal, was somehow awkward and Cocoa commented.

"Jack, are you listening to me?"

"Yeah, I'm just replaying everything in my head."

Cocoa grunted curtly. "I feel like I'm talking to myself, here. If I wanted that, I could've let that clown put you in jail."

"Cocoa, you didn't keep me from going to jail. In fact, if President Chamberlain hadn't shown up, we'd both be in jail."

"Whatever." In that moment, Cocoa thought of herself as Agent 99 and Jack as Maxwell Smart.

Jack noticed her expression. "But for real, I appreciate you stepping to Wahid for me. That was cool."

Cocoa gave in a little. "You know I couldn't let him roll up on you like that. Besides, who would I kick it with if you're behind bars in a dungeon?"

Jack cheshired. "So we're kicking it now, huh?"

"Don't get happy, big boy. Just a figure of speech."

They turned to head down a side street leading to their building and stopped in amazement. Cars were patiently waiting while an increasing group of thirty to forty men knelt in the middle of the street saying prayers.

"What time is it Jack?"

"Eleven thirty-five. Why?"

"I've never seen anything like this. It's…it's beautiful."

"It is pretty incredible to see this anywhere; but especially with the bad rap Muslims get at home for being ultra-violent. It's crazy 'cause I feel safer here than in L.A."

Cocoa agreed. "True. That's why travel is so cool. You see that everything is deeper than you thought. You mind if we watch until they finish?"

"Naw, girl. We're just kicking it, remember?"

With that, Cocoa let out a coy chuckle and gave her full attention to the praying men. As the time inched closer to midnight, others steadily joined the vigil until it seemed no more could fit into the formation. Some wore white garments to their ankles, others had on knit khakis and polo-style shirts. No one appeared conscious of what they had on or what the person next to them looked like. Even though there were no women, Cocoa still appreciated the gathering as a demonstration of the teaching power of religion.

Raised Catholic, she understood that Christians preferred to pray apart from each other, even if the principles of Mother Church taught otherwise. In the Bronx, their brand of Catholicism was infused with Latin culture. Mass for them was spirited and lively, to the degree that they got the nickname 'Catholic Pentecostals' because her church embraced tambourine playing and speaking in tongues. For Cocoa, Jesus wasn't a meek and lowly guy from Galilee. He was a trash-talking Esse from the barrio who had love for his people. This street praying felt like the radical faith stoking the fires of her survival instincts.

As the leader stood to his feet, the crowd imitated. Cars resumed, following the congregants making their way down the half-paved street.

"C'mon Cocoa, I need to tell Scribe that the fuzz has my phone and probably the file I sent him."

"Okay. Get some soda and chips from that vendor. Early dinner wore off too early for me. I'll be there in a minute."

She bent down to tie her shoe and Jack turned toward a storefront that looked like it had too many goods stocked on the shelves. It appeared that one more pack of candy or bag of Doritos would cause the whole shop to come crashing down like a house of cards. Buying a few items was Jack's Good Samaritan deed for the day. It would relieve pressure from the straining shelves plus win him some cool points with Cocoa.

Pocketing his change, Jack's stomach wrenched when he eyed a dark van curbside where he'd been standing. No Cocoa, but he was positive he saw kicking feet being yanked into the van.

"Help!" Cocoa's accent rang out.

Jack dropped the food and sprinted toward the vehicle. Cocoa managed to hook the backs of her knees onto the side panel, preventing the door from closing. Jack could see a large man holding a white handkerchief over her mouth and dragging her like a ragdoll. Before he could reach the van, her thrashing slowed and her body headed toward limpness.

"Oh God." Jack moaned, picking up speed.

He was ten yards away when the van door slammed shut, placing a metal barrier between him and the reason he chose to go to Egypt instead of Spain. Jack choked the neck of the mirror near the passenger window.

"Let her out now!"

The Embassy warned them to be careful because young, foreign women had recently been targeted by cartels who sold them as sex slaves on the underground market. Sometimes if women were traveling alone or in pairs, they would be lured to some destination or followed to their residence before abduction. If traveling with a male companion, the man would either be killed or distracted while the women were kidnapped. Either way, if the women were not found within twenty four hours, there was usually no hope of ever seeing them again.

Thoughts swarming like mosquitoes, Jack wailed and smashed through the glass with his fist and forearm. His eyes immediately darted to the back of the van where Cocoa lay unconscious and unmoving. Scrambling for the lock, a piece of glass dug into his wrist, causing him to haunch his shoulders. As he pulled up the lock with two fingers, Jack peered into the glowering eyes of a hooded figure robed in black who shifted the van into gear and sped off, causing Jack to tumble spine first onto the concrete street.

THIRTY THREE

Scribe could hear his mother say, *"Boy close your mouth before something flies in it."* For the first time, he really understood what she meant.

Mari and Scribe breathed in Chamberlain's words and Scribe held his mouth agape in apology. Mari pointed hard in his face, then gave him a wordless pat on the shoulder before moving around him to sit with Chamberlain.

Scribe broke the silence. "I guess that explains your Jose Conseco routine on these pictures."

Mari shot him a menacing cop look. "It was a kneejerk reaction. Anybody could have done it." She rubbed Chamberlain's back. "I called Delores because she was the only person I knew Lamir might not be watching closely."

Chamberlain patted Mari's leg. "I just went crazy when I saw all these pictures. It should have been me up there, not her."

"I didn't know you and Rock were *involved*", Scribe offered as more of a question than a statement.

"We weren't. Not like I wanted to be anyway. We'd done a dinner or two at my request, but he never suggested follow up encounters. So I slowed on the pursuit to give him some space. But when he told me he was headed to Egypt for two years, I blew my top. After I found out about this other woman, I felt lied to." Chamberlain looked down into her hands.

"But you said you weren't involved." Scribe knew he sounded like a typical man milliseconds after the words came out.

"Well my heart was involved, and that's all I needed to feel that way. He hadn't actually deceived me, but it still hurt. I was so angry that I wanted to get back at him."

Scribe's jaw tightened. "So you paid somebody to rough him up a bit?"

"No. I called the President of AUC and told him that Matthew was still under contract with Westerville and therefore obligated to return after the conclusion of the Spring semester. I figured Matthew would leave his little girlfriend behind and we could pick up where we left off."

"So when did you find out he was dead?"

"During my layover connecting to Cairo. A friend in the Police Department called me when he found out that Matthew taught at Westerville. I almost missed my flight because I was crying in the airport bathroom and couldn't hear the PA system."

Scribe nodded knowingly.

"During this trip, I was going to confront him with the information and pictures Mari took, tell him my true feelings, and that all was forgiven. But I never got the chance."

Mari spoke after a considerate pause. "Is this friend on the police force Lamir Wahid?"

"No. Khalim Habash."

Scribe searched Mari's reaction and she indicated who Habash was by saluting.

"This is the third year we've done this concert on our Mideast tour. There is another set of students in Tel Aviv living in a kibbutz and taking classes at the University. So I've developed a good working relationship with both the Cairo and Tel Aviv Police Departments. Chief Habash takes care of us when we're here. I'd just spoken to him the day before about security for the event so I wasn't surprised to hear from him when he called." Chamberlain shrugged. "In fact, he's the one who put me in contact with Mari."

Mari bobbed her head. "I wondered how you secured my information. Yet, I was thankful for the income, so I did not give it too much thought."

"Chief Habash spoke highly of your abilities and I liked the fact that you were a woman. Still I wanted my identity to remain secret."

"This is common. I understand."

"Well I don't." Scribe chimed in. "Sorry to interrupt your appreciation fest, but I'm still cloudy on why Rock was murdered."

Chamberlain wrung her hands. "That's why I agreed to come by and help. I feel I owe Matthew that much; especially since I tried to destroy what might have been true love for him. When Mari told me that the young lady had been strangled, my heart ached. Still, after I arrived and saw all these pictures…my only thought was, even in death, he'd chosen her over me."

Scribe empathized with Chamberlain and offered a counter position. "Dr. Chamberlain, I believe Rock knew we needed you here to find out why all this happened. It's hard to explain, but I feel like Rock has been urging me toward everything I've experienced for the past two days. But if I wouldn't have missed my first flight, maybe he'd still be alive."

Chamberlain waved him off. "Scribe, it's not your fault. It's nobody's fault but the sorry sack that killed my Matthew. And I want whoever did it to suffer like he did."

There was implicit agreement in the room.

Her demeanor turned professional. "So tell me about these Bible verses he emailed you." Chamberlain had studied Political Science on the graduate level but made a choice between that and Harvard Divinity School. She elected to focus on terrestrial entities instead of metaphysical ones, but was still sharp when it came to Christian theology; which was the initial connection between her and Rockman.

After a moment, Scribe returned from the computer holding three printouts with notes scribbled in the margins.

"Okay, from Jack's translation I managed to find the corresponding verses while Mari slept. They're all from the four Gospels of the New Testament. I made a copy for each of you." He passed them around like class handouts. "I have a theory but first I want to hear what you both think."

They each read silently:

Matthew 12:40: 'For as Jonah was three days and three nights in the whale's belly; so shall the Son of man be three days and three nights in the heart of the earth.'

Matthew 16:21: 'From that time on, Jesus began to explain to his disciples that he must go to Jerusalem and suffer greatly at the hands of the elders and chief priests, and be killed, and on the third day be raised.'

John 19:30: 'When Jesus tasted the vinegar he said "It is finished", bowed his head, and gave up his spirit.'

John 19:31: 'Since it was the day of Preparation, in order to prevent the bodies from hanging on the cross on the Sabbath—because that was a High Sabbath—the Jews requested Pilate to have the legs broken and the body taken away.'

Luke 23:55: 'The women who had come with him from Galilee followed, and they saw the tomb and how his body was laid.'

Mark 16:1: 'When the Sabbath was over, Mary Magdalene, Mary the mother of James, and Salome bought spices so they might go and anoint him.'

Luke 23:56: 'Then they returned, and prepared spices and ointments. On the Sabbath day they rested according to the commandment.'

John 20:1: 'Early on the first day of the week, while it was still dark, Mary Magdalene came to the tomb and saw that the stone had been removed.'

When Mari and Chamberlain lifted their eyes they found Scribe searching their expressions, pressing the paper to his lips in anticipation. Before either could speak, a booming knock at the door shook the thin walls of Rockman's hideout.

"Open up. Cairo Police." It was a young voice. Not brusque or raspy like Wahid's, but possessing a feigned forcefulness that sounded more assumed than authoritative.

"Just a minute", Chamberlain sang, motioning for Scribe and Mari to head into the bedroom. Silently, they crammed into the sleeping area feeling trapped, but marveling at Chamberlain's levelheadedness.

Chamberlain took a deep breath, mussed her hair, and opened the door.

THIRTY FOUR

Jack heard the humming of an approaching car. There were no headlights, just a vibrating tone that grew closer as he lie bleeding at the corner of a building blocking his view of oncoming traffic. Though the storefronts were lit, it was midnight and Cairo drivers treated dark, deserted streets like the Audubon.

The small white Datsun barreling toward Jack sported a hood that appeared to have been the landing pad for a thousand pound guerilla with dirty feet. The disfigured grill clung to the frame by hanger wire, yet still managed to resemble the face of a snarling pit bull.

All Jack could do was roll left. It was just enough to avoid the worn tire tread leaving a stripe on his stomach. He panted while righting himself, astonished that no one had batted an eye in the last minute to help him or Cocoa. The people nearby noticed him, but not in a concerned way. They were paying attention, but absently; like people at a bus stop watching someone's car being towed. For Jack's onlookers, his plight came closer to sad entertainment than anything worth caring about.

Before Jack and Cocoa caught their flight to Egypt, the group had a meeting with an exchange student from Cairo who gave them the cultural do's and don'ts.

"For the most part Cairo is a modern city that has both traditional and cosmopolitan elements, but they coexist in harmony." Fyso was laid back and easygoing, so that description of Cairo was plausible coming from him.

"Check out the souks and try to make it to Aswan if you can. It's burning hot but, in the early morning, you can see the Nile in its natural state without all the smog and skyscrapers. If you get homesick, the American Embassy is about a mile walk from your hotel. They get their mustard from France, but they still use two all-beef patties and a sesame seed bun."

Rick and Terry high-fived each other and Jack rocked like he had on headphones. He was a Burger King man himself, twice a day when his refund money was right, but McDonald's would do in a pinch.

For some reason, Cocoa felt that Fyso wasn't providing enough information and made that plain.

"Fyso, as the only woman in the group, I want to know if there will be any static if I don't wear a scarf on my head or long skirts everyday?"

Fyso took a swig of his Coke and answered. "You should be okay, unless you're going into a mosque. So take a skirt and scarf in your book bag just in case."

"So you're saying that nobody is going to trip because I wear pants or shorts?"

"Well, you may get some winks from the married men and frowns from their wives, but most people will see you as American and won't even notice. Don't worry, Cocoa, they'll love you and everything will be fine."

Cocoa cocked her head to the side and waved her hand. "Good, because I'd hate to have to whip a butt in the middle of the street."

Fyso's eyes stretched and he deliberately placed his drink down onto the table. "Cocoa, this is very important and I need you to listen to me."

Cocoa straightened her back and gave him her full attention, lips pursed.

"Under no circumstances should you raise your voice at an Egyptian man on the street. In the Muslim world this is seen as disrespectful and I have witnessed women beaten while policemen stood to watch before taking the woman to jail. I know this is most extraordinary but please be careful not to do this."

Smacking her lips, Cocoa leaned back in her seat and chortled, "Whatever."

Nursing the cuts near his elbow, Jack wondered if this had anything to do with an unknown street altercation between Cocoa and some macho loon. Cocoa's participation in something like that was so possible that it was probable. Jack didn't know what to think and hurried past the disinterested bystanders conducting business as usual.

Blood trickled down his arm at a moderate pace and he needed to get the biggest cut wrapped to stop the bleeding. It wasn't deep enough for stitches, yet the length of it created a large enough canal for blood to flow rapidly. The glass hadn't hit a vein, nevertheless the jagged edge sliced a good chunk of flesh when Hood Master tore way from the curb.

Jack applied pressure to the wound and let his mind wander back to a scene he and Cocoa witnessed last week walking from work. There was a skulking crowd forcibly escorting a lone man down the sidewalk. After a few paces, the prisoner protested and tried to stop his forward momentum by swinging and kicking. The group proceeded to thrash him into obedience until he yielded. Regrouping, the mob continued their march until locating a police car. One of them opened the back door and the mob threw their captive in. Another told the officer what the prisoner had done and the officer sped off, presumably to take the man to jail.

Citizen's arrest was one thing, but that smacked of vigilante justice. Jack could only hope that Cocoa's kidnapper would be found before he had a chance to hurt her. Running and bleeding with a card in his hand, he had to get some professional help from the only guy he knew who had enough clout to find Cocoa before it was too late.

THIRTY FIVE

A smooth faced man in uniform stood with a flashlight in his hand. Looking down at Chamberlain, he gathered himself and began.

"Madam, do you live here?" He figured he knew the answer but decided to ask anyway.

"No, my friends do."

"Who might that be, ma'am?"

"Rabbi Rockman, Rabbi Goethe, and Rabbi…Fowsta." Chamberlain prayed that Officer Indo was not up on his German literature.

"Rockman? Was he not killed a few nights ago?"

"Yes. I came from the U.S. as soon as I heard." Indo nodded, but still had the scowl of the Grand Inquisitor.

"Well ma'am, I am here because we had a complaint about noise coming from this unit. Next door the neighbors said they heard the sound of breaking glass and crying, so I am here to investigate. May I come in?"

Chamberlain had to make a split second decision that appeared natural.

"First let me explain the sounds the neighbors heard. The breaking glass and crying was me. See…when I arrived and saw pictures of Matthew, I became so overwhelmed that I lost it for a minute. When I snapped out of my trance, I'd broken almost every piece of glass in the place. Some people eat, other people break things. I'm a breaker."

She smiled and Indo pretended to jot Chamberlain's story down while peeking over her head into the apartment. He couldn't see any shards of glass but sudden movements in the rear caught his eye.

"Ma'am, I need you to step aside while I search the premises." Indo firmly rested his hand on Chamberlain's shoulder and moved forward.

Her eyes locked onto his chest and she snapped. "Touching me in that way is inappropriate, Officer Indo. I would hate to report this to Chief Habash."

Indo backed up. He had almost been on the job six months and went up for his semi-annual review next week. The fact that Chamberlain even knew the Chief's name gave him pause. He'd heard stories of rookies that got on the Chief's bad side and never made it to their annual review. Indo couldn't let that happen to him.

"Touching you in what way, ma'am? I was only doing my job."

"Is your job to sexually assault me?" Chamberlain put both hands on her hips.

"Miss…?"

"Doctor. Dr. Delores Chamberlain", she corrected.

"Dr. Chamberlain. I apologize for the misunderstanding. I placed my hand on your shoulder to alert you that I was moving forward and to maintain a safe distance between us. It was not my intention to cause you any discomfort or behave suggestively."

Chamberlain pursed her lips, then shot back. "If I were in traditional Muslim garb, would you have touched me?"

Indo was speechless. The answer was certainly no, but to say that aloud would tighten the sling he already found himself in. Chamberlain worked hard not to look back, hoping that she'd bought Scribe and Mari enough time to hide or climb out a back window.

Again Indo saw movement in the apartment behind Chamberlain. He had been at the University with the forensics team in charge of Adeena's murder, taping off the area and preventing curious students from wandering into the crime scene. The security guard reported that the suspects ran in this direction and there were two officers in the area questioning local residents. He calculated the risks to his career if he was wrong, but he had a hunch. When the call came in from the neighbors, Indo sprinted over.

"Ma'am, step aside please."

"Do you have a warrant?"

"No, but I have probable cause that two suspects for a murder committed at AUC could be hiding here and that you are aiding and abetting these fugitives."

This time Chamberlain was speechless. Before she could react, Indo drew his weapon and pushed past her.

Once inside, he saw the glass and fallen picture frames littering the room. Surveying the terrain, Indo radioed the beat cops walking the area.

"Possible location of suspects at Zamalek Residence, Unit one, two, four, zero. Officer requesting backup."

Inching like a ninja, Indo heard muffled voices coming from the dimly lit bedroom. The only scenarios close to this for him were in the Academy when he knew the people in the next room had blanks in their guns. Judging from the havoc wreaked upon that college girl earlier tonight, if these guys had guns, they definitely wouldn't be filled with blanks. With his back against the wall and gun in prayer position, Indo neared the end of a mental three-count; after which he planned to yell for the occupants to come out with their hands up. Having counted two, he heard a voice.

"Delores, are you prepared to leave?"

The voice was slurred and Transylvanian, not quite high pitched but by no means heavy.

Indo pivoted to glance into the eyes of a catatonic Chamberlain.

To her amazement, an elderly man of medium height and build came strolling out of the bedroom, dressed in a long black bekishe and a shtreimel made of sable fur covering his entire head. His beard was thick like ivy coiling over his mouth and hanging down to the collar of his robe.

Following the distress in Chamberlain's gaze, the man angled his body to face a befuddled Officer Indo holding his revolver with both hands.

Raising his thin fingers the man intoned, "What is the meaning of this?"

Indo relaxed and tried to hide his weapon. "One thousand apologies, Rabbi. I was searching for suspects in a recent murder and had reason to believe they were here."

"May I lower my hands officer?"

"Yes, sir. Of course."

"Is everything all right out here?" Another voice, deeper and smoothly baritone, floated from the hidden nook.

A taller man emerged from the bedroom similarly attired. Younger, he had less facial hair than his mentor, but it was fine and shiny, lying on his cheeks like satin. His bekishe stopped just below the knees, however his dark slacks and the fact that he only peeked out from the waist up hid this fact. The silk, black stripes on his biceps indicated that he was an Orthodox Rabbinic Scholar with high visibility in Judaism. Indo's first official assignment had been to chauffeur Jewish delegates from the airport to an academic summit at the University in January, and he'd noted the ranking distinctions.

"Everything is fine, Rabbi. I was just telling your friend how a misunderstanding caused your inconvenience."

"Yes, I am ready to go." Chamberlain's bearings had returned and she resumed her role in the play. "Since there are murderers on the loose, I will be sure to tell Chief Habash of your courtesy in escorting us safely to our car."

Indo's top lip quivered as Chamberlain ended her statement with a patronizing smirk. He holstered his gun and reached for his shoulder, depressing the communicator button. "Cancel that last call."

THIRTY SIX

The black Mercedes Benz inched up to the police barricade and paused to roll down the window. The officer on duty held a photo of Scribe and Mari captured from surveillance cameras at police headquarters. Looking past Chamberlain, all he saw were two rabbis in the backseat. Not much chance of Scribe and Mari hiding under their feet.

"Ma'am, could you open your trunk please?"

Chamberlain pretended to consider the request and then replied, "Yes, but why?"

"We have fugitives on the loose and this is a routine procedure."

She hit the button on her left console and the trunk rose like Dracula's coffin lid. After a few waves of his flashlight, the officer returned to the driver side window. *Odd*, he thought, because he knew most of the people in the area and he'd surely have remembered two rabbis. From the periphery of his right eye, a figure approached with a telephone to his ear.

"She's a friend of the Chief. I've got Inspector Wahid on the phone and he verified it, so let them through." After watching the duty guard signal for the cones to be removed, Indo ran in the other direction.

When she heard the familiar voice Chamberlain's window rose, the barricade parted, and the Benz slowly blended into the distant night. Chamberlain had joked to Ms. Wash before boarding her flight that if a woman played her cards right, the male ego could be manipulated and might even come in handy every now and then. Officer Indo was a case in point. She threw her head back against the headrest, belly laughed, and punched the accelerator.

"Way to go girlfriend." Chamberlain winked into her rearview mirror at Mari.

"Thank you. I could not have done it if you had not delayed him at the door."

Scribe chimed in. "I guess your thespian and detective combination makes you a master of disguises. If I didn't know it was me, I wouldn't recognize myself in a mirror."

Mari blushed. "At least my training is good for something. Even though there were only five or six people, that's the biggest audience I've ever had."

"Is it safe to take all this off? I'm sweating like a pig."

Mari chided. "No. We must stay in character in case we are being followed."

Chamberlain harrumphed. "You know, you may be sweating but not like a pig, because pigs don't sweat. Let's say you're sweating like a man who owes his freedom to two women and has not thanked them yet."

Touché, Scribe thought. "Thank you ladies for saving me. I definitely couldn't have made it without you." He let them gloat and inhale his gratitude before adding, "So what are your thoughts on the verses?"

Mari answered first after she pulled the printout from her pocket. "The first two verses state that when Jesus is crucified, he will spend three complete days and nights in the grave before rising from the dead; like Jonah spent in the whale before being released. My dad used to tell me that story all the time. We didn't talk too much about Jesus, though."

Mari pressed Scribe. "What do you think about the story, David?"

"Not much really. I enjoyed it, but that's about it. I can't really say I believed that a guy camped out in a whale for three days until he was spouted out onto dry land. Still I did imagine him sitting on a stool around a campfire until the whale spat him out."

"I think we all did." Chamberlain joined. "But the idea seems to be that Jonah was an Old Testament Jesus who dies for three days and, in some sense, comes back to life. Do you concur, Professor?"

"Indeed, I do. I see Harvard Divinity lost a fine pupil when you turned them down."

Chamberlain countered, "Well a girl's got to do..." She gestured for the chorus to complete her statement. "At that time, the boys weren't giving much ground in the Church, but the glass ceiling was starting to crack in education and politics. That's where I saw my future and...here I am. But I do still miss it, the scholarship."

Scribe understood. "I'm sure. And you definitely have a knack for it." Chamberlain monitored her speed, knowing that female drivers were uncommon in much of the Arab world.

He resumed. "So does anything strike you as odd about the first two verses?" He'd put on his professor's cap and settled into the Socratic method.

Chamberlain remained with the thought. "Not off hand. Jonah stayed in the whale's belly for three days and Jesus was crucified on Friday and resurrected on Sunday; three days."

He glanced over. "Mari, any thoughts?"

Mari shrugged. "Sounds fine to me."

Scribe moaned agreement. "It does sound fine…until you think beyond how it sounds." Scribe presumed from their silence that he still had the floor. "Dr. Chamberlain, let's say you agreed to pay me $1,000 after I had worked at Westerville for three days."

She nodded, checking her side mirrors.

"Let's also say that I began working Friday evening and appeared at your home before dawn on Sunday morning and demanded my money. What would you say to me?"

Chamberlain didn't respond. After calculating, Mari did. "I would say come back Monday night because you have only worked one day and a half."

"Exactly." Scribe said smiling at Mari.

Chamberlain cleared her throat. "As kids we used to wonder how you got three days out of Friday night to Sunday morning, but all the adults seemed content with the chronology and, eventually, we got used to it, too."

"True." His tone shifted into a Southern Baptist minster. "What would an Easter sermon be if the preacher didn't lay Jesus in the grave on Friday night and whoop him alive early Sunday morning?"

They laughed and Scribe made his point. "But if we treat these texts as true, then the Friday to Sunday resurrection scenario can't be right…and Rock obviously knew that."

Chamberlain swerved on the brakes and pulled the car over to a shoulder adjacent to the Nile River. "So what exactly are you saying?" She craned her neck and Mari stared at him intently.

"I'm saying I think the reason Rock was killed is because he figured out something about the resurrection that his killer didn't want him to share. And I think the answer is in these verses he emailed me."

Simultaneously they each refocused on their copy, hoping a message would emerge if they stared long and hard enough.

Chamberlain darted out of the driver's seat and opened the backdoor, sandwiching Scribe between herself and Mari. "If they killed Matthew over this, then we're going to sit here until we figure it out."

There was no argument from Mari or Scribe; especially since she had both the car keys and the fury of a Wild West gunslinger in her eyes.

Chamberlain proceeded. "Okay, in the third verse Jesus dies. That's clear. But what is this about 'the day of Preparation' and a 'High Sabbath'?"

Scribe swiveled to Mari. "Help us out here."

Reticently Mari admitted, "I haven't heard those terms since childhood. But the Day of Preparation was when we assembled everything we needed for the next day since it was forbidden to do any work or cooking on the Sabbath. Only certain activities were permitted, like going to Temple or spending time with your family."

Chamberlain urged. "Makes sense. But what's the difference between a regular Sabbath and a High Sabbath?"

Mari mimed like she'd just remembered that part of the question. "Oh yes, a High Sabbath is a very special day in Judaism that marks a sacred occasion like Yom Kippur or, in this case, the first day of The Feast of Unleavened Bread. It can occur on a regular Sabbath or on any other day of the week. It just depends on the calendar. I remember because when a High Sabbath came before or after a regular one, that made two consecutive days that I wasn't allowed to go out and play." She smiled but recalling the memory made her relive days of solitary confinement.

Chamberlain crinkled her tear ducts in thought. "Humph. This verse says Jesus was crucified on the day of Preparation and the next day was a High Sabbath. For the record, Jewish days begin and end at 6pm, right?"

Mari nodded. "Right, from evening to evening."

"Okay. I knew that but, not knowing what a High Sabbath was, I always assumed it was a regular Friday evening to Saturday evening Sabbath. But if a High Sabbath can be any day of the week, the question seems to be on what day of the week was this particular High Sabbath?"

Scribe was impressed and followed the volley back to Mari. "Can't we just get a Jewish calendar and do some calculations to find out?"

He broke in to the thought. "We could, but we don't know in which year all this supposedly happened. All the common dates we use for Jesus' life are approximations so a calendar won't help us much unless we know the exact week and year we're looking for."

Chamberlain added, "We know the week is Passover week, we just don't know the year."

Scribe contributed at that point. "We also know that Jesus was betrayed and taken in the Garden on the actual day of Passover. Remember, the Lord's Supper was the Passover meal they ate in the beginning of the day, which would have been sometime after 6 pm."

Chamberlain followed. "That would mean he was crucified on the actual day of Passover, the latter half."

As an addendum to her statement, a faint beeping noise filled the air. Scribe gave Mari a knowing glance before he felt a familiar buzz on his own hip. More surprised than anything, he popped the phone off his belt and eyeballed the screen. Scribe rarely received calls since his wife died and probably touched the keys no more than five times a month. But his phone had world reception capability that he had forgotten about until that moment.

"Who is it?", Mari queried.

Shaking as he skimmed Jack's text message, the only word Scribe managed to blurt out was "Drive!"

THIRTY SEVEN

Cocoa awoke to the rumbling of an eight cylinder engine that hadn't had a tune-up since the day it rolled off the assembly line. Her cheek was cold and gritty, but when she went to wipe it, her discovery that she was hogtied explained why that desire could not be fulfilled.

Unexpectantly, the van rocked as if B.A. Baracus forgot to install shock absorbers before the A-Team getaway chase. The road surface had changed from normal potholes and cracks in the pavement to something like cobblestone or a pile of rubble left lying in the middle of the street. Cocoa felt like she was in the flatbed of a monster truck crushing junk cars with jackhammers strapped to the wheels.

The bare metal interior appeared corroded from the brown and orange splotches on the walls. The windows were draped with opaque grey cloth frayed at the edges. Two cushioned seats stood bolted to the floor next to hard plastic cabinets that lined both side panels. Rifle racks adorned the back doors and dim overhead halogens shone down from the ceiling.

Turning counter-clockwise on her hip, Cocoa felt like a break dancer peering at the back of the driver's head and the cloak that hung down to his ankles. He wore sandals and a pair of dark trousers underneath, concealing a bulge outside his right shin.

"Hey, let me out of here!"

Stopping at a traffic light, the driver looked over his shoulder, turned back, and gave the idling engine some gas. Cocoa saw dried blood staining the ear fringe of his hood.

Even with the roar of the engine, his heavy tone was terrifying because it was so dismissive. "Your friends think they are so clever, but they know nothing."

Most people would've dived out of the van headfirst into oncoming traffic to get away from such a brooding figure. Not Cocoa.

"What are you talking about fool?"

Without turning, the keeper responded. "I regret it has come to this, but in every war there are civilian casualties."

"When I get untied, I'll show you some casualties. The first one will be my foot broke off in your…"

"Silence woman!"

Cocoa paused partially from being startled and partially from outrage. "Silence? You don't tell me…"

The van came to a screeching halt. The Keeper gripped the steering wheel but remained still, facing forward. Cocoa inhaled breaths so quickly she could smell the rusting metal floorboard beneath the rubber traction mat. She took a second look at the bulge in his pants leg and thought better of continuing her objection.

Satisfied, the Keeper pressed the accelerator and the van lurched forward.

Wahid told Jack it would be forty-five minutes before he could come and take his statement. He suggested that other officers could respond sooner, but Jack only wanted to deal with Wahid.

As a consequence, Jack refused to relay anything but broad details of the kidnapping until Wahid arrived to hear it for himself.

When he wasn't studying, Jack was a television and movieholic. Crime and thrillers mostly. Because of it, he developed an attitude toward lower level police officers as often incompetent and always powerless. Jack knew every minute was precious and affected Cocoa's safe return but, in his mind, without the complaint being acted upon at a high enough level, nothing meaningful would happen anyway. So the extra thirty minutes he decided to wait on Wahid was time well spent.

When Wahid finally arrived, an hour and a half had passed since their initial conversation. Jack was sitting in the lobby of his apartment building favoring the forearm he'd wrapped in an ace bandage. Wahid wore a windbreaker that read "Shorta" on the back and the left breast. A badge embroidered with gold and black translated the word for any tourists, even from a distance.

"What happened to you?", Wahid began.

"I could ask you the same question. What took you so long?"

"My apologies. The things I had to wrap up took longer than I expected. Mr. Jack, you do realize that it is 2am, do you not?"

Jack flinched and shifted on the sofa away from his injuries, scowling. "I know that, man. But this is life and death here."

Wahid perched next to Jack and flipped open a pad before dryly exhaling, "Start from the beginning and tell me anything you can remember."

Jack recounted everything that happened, even the things that occurred before the incident. Wahid didn't look up once. One time Jack paused and asked if Wahid was listening. Wahid stoically replied, "Uh huh", and motioned with his fingers for Jack to keep going. When Jack finished he breathlessly posed a question. "Well?"

"Well what?"

"Well what do you think?"

Wahid raised his head and closed the tablet. "I think you should get some rest and have your wounds examined."

Jack gritted his teeth. "What are you going to do to help Cocoa?"

"The first thing I will do is call a medic and get your arm attended to. Next I will post an officer near your door and two outside this building to protect you in case the abductor returns to finish the job."

"None of that's going to help get Cocoa back."

"No. But it will help keep you safe and contain the damage from spiraling any further."

As if on cue, a plain clothes Officer Indo, dressed like a college student, walked up to Wahid and stood awaiting his instructions.

"Take Mr. Jack to his apartment and make sure no one goes in or out unless I give the order."

Jack lunged at Wahid, grabbed his collar with his bruised arm, and yelled into his ear. "You'd better find Cocoa or you'll be sorry!"

Wahid slapped Jack's arm away causing Jack to slide down the windbreaker, falling to one knee. Jack groaned clutching his arm while Indo hesitated, witnessing blood seep through the fibers of the ace bandage.

Wahid exclaimed, "Call the medic and get him to his apartment now!"

The underling Indo snatched Jack up by his good arm, hustling him into the elevator with unnecessary roughness.

THIRTY EIGHT

Wahid arrived at the scene of Cocoa's abduction and questioned some of the merchants about what had happened. None of them remembered anything, not even Jack running or dropping his snacks on the ground. The vendors had an unspoken pact: don't talk to the cops and your store won't be burned down when you come back tomorrow. Somebody could be drawn and quartered while they all sat on their stoops and drank tea. Unless the victim was a relative, the police could count on colliding with a wall of silence.

"So Raja, do you remember an American here around midnight?"

Raja looked more like a Sumo than a shopkeeper. He weighed at least 450 pounds and sported a bald head that would've made Kojak jealous. "Indeed. He bought chips and then ran away."

"Did you see where he went?"

"No. He left and went toward the street." Raja pointed to the left. "I did not see him after that."

Wahid glared at him. "What about the girl?"

"No girl. Only him."

"And the van?"

"What van?" Raja twiddled his thumbs atop the counter.

Wahid gave him a card that he was sure would end up in the bottom of a trashcan before long. "Call me if you think of anything else."

Wahid knew Raja was lying, but it didn't matter. What he wanted to know, he learned through Raja's nonchalance. He also spotted traces of blood at the intersection that moved in the direction Jack described. In most abduction cases, not much could be done until the kidnappers communicated their demands. If they wanted something more than they wanted the mark, the victim had a better chance of surviving. But if they only wanted the girl, she was either sold or dead already. Wahid was certain his visit ensured that he could count on Raja's silence if anyone else came asking about the incident.

By the time Wahid realized Jack had picked his pocket, he was finishing with Raja and climbing into his cruiser. Posing as Jack, he'd sent Scribe a text message about Cocoa's kidnapping to flush him out of hiding. But before Scribe responded, Jack had swiped the phone. Luckily, the tech guy installed an electronic monitoring device that displayed all correspondence to and from Jack's Blackberry on Wahid's. The message he just received meant the tech guy would get his annual raise after all.

After the medic left, Jack woke Rick and Terry and filled them in on the situation, including their de facto house arrest.

Terry spoke first. "We gotta do something."

"What are we supposed to do, kill the police outside the door so we can go God-knows-where to hunt down some kidnappers in a foreign country? Please. Rick ain't getting murdered for nobody."

Jack clenched his fists. "Rick, you're such a punk. Wahid is trying to play us and Cocoa is running out of time. If we don't help her, who will?"

"Jack, don't act all brand new. I know that's your little girlfriend, but why don't you let the police handle their business and get Cocoa back?"

"Rick, I swear, if anything happens to her…"

"Guys!" Terry jumped between them and put one hand on each of their chests. "We can't do this, not now." He turned. "Rick, get over it man. Cocoa needs us. You know she'd be the first one to help if it were you."

Jack continued gritting his teeth, even after Rick had backed down. Rick's shoulders slumped as he sat at the kitchen table and exhaled. "My bad fellas. I just got scared for a minute. I know, I know. We've gotta do something, but what?"

Jack still wanted to punch him in the nose to release some anxiety. But he accepted his apology by answering the question. "We need a diversion."

Terry chimed in. "Like what?"

Jack waved his hands like a quarterback forming a huddle and whispered, "Here's what we'll do…"

Chamberlain valeted at the Semiramis and strolled across the foyer accompanied by the two rabbis. Their gait was purposeful but even, and no one but the front desk attendant saw them enter the elevator. In the car, Scribe had paraphrased the gist of Cocoa's abduction and his request for Jack to meet them at the hotel. He urged Chamberlain to call the American Embassy but she refused, wanting to wait until the police had a chance to resolve the matter quietly. Scribe objected, yet realized he was in no position to march up to the authorities and demand anything. So they'd decided the best thing was to get off the streets and that no one would think to look for them in the place they had just escaped.

When they reached the top floor, Scribe let an "ooh" escape his lips before catching himself. Chamberlain's suite made his look like a Chicago Housing Project. In addition to his, hers had a living area, fully stocked bar, a wall mounted television, and a fresh water aquarium brimming with brilliant coral, exotic fish, and vibrant plant life. The Jacuzzi built for two sat adjacent to a fireplace capable of either faux or real flames upon request. Chamberlain claimed the armchair and motioned for Mari and Scribe to take the sofa.

Chamberlain began. "What time did Jack say he would meet us here?"

"He didn't. But, if I know Jack, it won't be too long."

"What about Rick and Terry? How reliable are they?"

Scribe grinned. "They're kind of like Scooby and Shaggy, loyal but needing lots of guidance."

Mari didn't follow the joke. "Sadly lots of young women are kidnapped in the Middle East so there is no way to know if this is related to the other deaths or merely random misfortune."

"Not on the surface, but something tells me that it's all connected." Scribe studied the pensive Chamberlain before going out on a limb. "Dr. Chamberlain, do you believe in the Afterlife?"

Chamberlain clasped her fingers and peered into Scribe's intentions. "I guess so. I believe in Christ's resurrection, but I've never thought much about personal immortality." Chamberlain followed a reflective pause with her own question. "Why do you ask?"

Scribe counted the costs and plunged forward. "I know this might sound strange, but I believe Rock has been contacting me from the other side."

The silence magnified the rattle from the central air vents. Scribe started at his Pyramid dream and recounted his other experiences, from Gloria to the voice at St. George's Church.

"But it wasn't just that." His eyes widened. "It's been the nagging intuitions that have convinced me more than anything. They're more like feelings than information, but they go beyond language. It's like somebody cutting you open and placing a deeper understanding about a thing inside of you. You don't know how it got there or maybe even what it means, but you know it's there."

Chamberlain nodded. "I think I understand. It's like babies knowing how to breast feed without being taught. Or more like knowing you shouldn't take the D-Train today and then hearing about a gunman who killed five people on your route."

"Yeah, like that." Scribe leaned forward. "Well, I feel like Rock has been helping me and wants me to make things right. I don't really know how to do that, but I know these verses are the key."

Mari touched his shoulder. "So you think the killer kidnapped Cocoa?"

"Yes, I do. And I know the only bargaining chip we have is to figure out the message Rock left us. Otherwise, the killer has no motivation to keep Cocoa alive."

Chamberlain picked up the telephone receiver. "Then we'd better order room service."

THRITY NINE

The door to Jack's apartment creaked wide. Officer Indo, asleep on a chair in the hallway, jerked awake at the sound. His eyes darted from the elevator to the stairwell door, thinking that his prisoners had sneaked past him and escaped. Once ruling that out, Indo stood at the apartment threshold with his blackjack ready and crept forward like a crouching tiger.

There was no way he could get promoted if he goofed an assignment given personally by Wahid. All he had to do was keep a group of college kids secure until the Inspector returned. That's it. Instead, he was facing the threat of getting fired when Wahid got back. If he had to split an American head open to keep that from happening, so be it.

The living room was small, surrounded by three bedrooms and a kitchen. Nothing on the counter but half a loaf of bread and a box of honey buns. When this little hide and seek adventure was over, Indo planned to swipe the pastries as a consolation prize for his trouble.

Beyond the kitchen wall, he saw that two of the bedroom doors were closed. Indo thought the element of surprise was better so he slowly peeked into each, finding them empty. The third door was cracked and lamplight faintly shone through the gap. Indo tiptoed toward the entrance and heard what sounded like muffled voices inside. For all he knew, they were planning their escape or plotting to attack him. But one good blackjack whack would end that conversation.

Bursting in, he hurriedly searched the room and saw a clock radio tuned to an English language talk show. But it was the fluttering sheet on the window sill that commanded his full attention. "Damn!"

Indo yanked a fistful of fabric, hoping his escapees were still dangling somewhere in the middle. To his surprise, when he leaned out the window, there was only one sheet tied to the bed railing. *How could they possibly climb down four stories with one sheet?*, he wondered. While Indo pondered how the front door had come ajar, his legs left the floor and he found himself dangling by his ankles along the rear wall of the apartment building.

Teary-voiced, Indo begged. "No, please. Put me down. I have a family!" He waved his arms wildly and his blackjack clanked against the concrete below.

Rick and Terry pulled him in a bit while Jack tied his ankles together, anchoring the sheet to the window handle and the cast iron bed frame bolted to the floor. Indo had walked right past Rick and Terry underneath the bed and Jack was hidden in the closet on the opposite side of the room. Jack's plan worked perfectly, but he didn't anticipate that Indo would be wailing like a child who had gone potty on himself.

Rick urged nervously. "Hurry up Jack. This guy's going to get us caught."

Jack finished the sailor's knot his uncle had shown him many years ago and yelled down to Indo, "Shut up or we'll drop you!"

Indo's shrieks turned to snivels and the three amigos dashed out the front door toward the elevator.

On the way down Terry blurted, "We could go to jail for this, Jack."

This time, Rick handled the panic. "We're in it now, Terry. Ride or die for Cocoa, remember?"

Jack remembered, too, but he'd tried to keep his mind off the dying part. So much time had passed since she was snatched that all he could think was the worst. So he stared at the digital display of descending floors without comment. They had to get to President Chamberlain and the Semiramis was only five blocks away. If they ran, they could be there in less than two minutes. But that might bring attention they really didn't need at this point. All of this went through Jack's mind as his brain tingled and the elevator took forever to reach the bottom. As soon as the doors opened, he would call the front desk and get connected to Chamberlain's room.

The sound of Michael Jackson's *PYT* filled the cavity of the elevator. It was his personalized ringtone for Cocoa's number. Jack wouldn't have been surprised if she'd trash-talked her way out of the situation or browbeat her abductor to the point that he released her for some peace and quiet. Nobody wanted to buy a female slave who would kill you in the middle of the night, no matter how beautiful she was. Still there was the possibility that she was somewhere hurt and needed his help fast.

He answered with a mixture of glee and concern. "Cocoa?"

The voice on the other end was deliberate and cold. "If you wish to see the girl again, have Scribe and Mari come to St. Sergius alone…or she will die like the Rabbi."

After that, the voice was gone and Jack pounded the elevator doors.

"What happened?", Terry and Rick said in unison.

"Man, we've got to get to that hotel fast."

When the doors opened, brawny uniformed officers caught the fleeing boys in bear hugs and wrestled them to the ground. They swung, but it was like the unpopular version of the Goliath story where David misses and gets crushed to death. The more they struggled, the tighter the ropes got around their wrists. Now they looked more like escaped goldfish bouncing up and down on their stomachs. Panting, Jack saw a familiar pair of loafers sauntering toward him through the front doors of the apartment building. The loafers' owner knelt down, flipped open a notepad, and scanned all three of their faces prior to remarking: "Hi guys. Going somewhere?"

The kitchen sent up their chicken salads in brushed silver bowls with ancient Pharaoh scenes etched in raised relief. The glamorous presentation made it almost improper to alter the salad in any way. Almost.

Chamberlain complimented the chef on the first bite. Scribe depicted his euphoria another way. "Now I know how John the Baptist must have felt at Herod's banquet before he received the bad news about his head."

Mari's slight pause between her second mouthful to giggle let Scribe know that she'd understood that one. Surprisingly she added, "If John had a salad like this in front of him at the time, he may not have seen the executioners standing over him."

Chamberlain snickered, noticing that Scribe's anecdotal humor was rubbing off on Mari. She put down her fork and wiped her mouth. "Okay Professor, you've heard what we have to say on the verses. What say you?"

Scribe licked salad greens from his teeth, turned toward Chamberlain, and opened his mouth. "To piggyback on your last point in the car, it would have to be right that Christ was crucified on the Passover. But the text also says that it was a Day of Preparation, but for what?"

Mari wiped her mouth. "I can help you there. The Passover and the Day of Preparation are one and the same. According to Leviticus 23, one of the Feasts that Jews are commanded to keep is the Feast of Unleavened Bread. It is a seven day feast that is preceded by the one-day commemoration of Passover, when Yahweh spared the first-born Jewish children before the Exodus." She swallowed, glad to contribute. "The first and seventh days of the Feast of Unleavened Bread are High Sabbaths, or special Sabbaths that can fall on any day of the week."

Scribe stared. "So the Day of Preparation and the Day of Passover are the same day?"

"Yes."

"Interesting." He held his fork, full of salad, in midair. "So for what exactly were they preparing?"

Mari covered her full mouth. "Originally it was the journey out of Egypt. But tradition encouraged a removal of all yeast from the home and we also killed…the Passover sacrificial lamb". Mari crinkled her nose at the awkward implication in the company of Christians.

Chamberlain placed a hand on Mari's knee. "The ultimate transubstantiation." Mari laughed appreciatively.

I think you've both brought the issue to a head with the 'Day of Preparation' and the 'High Sabbath'. We can't figure out those days because we don't know the year. But I think the key to the puzzle lies with the women."

Chamberlain came in on cue. “Honey, the key to everything in life lies with women.” Mari returned her nod with a wink. “But tell us how we unlock the mystery this time.”

Scribe smarted before continuing. “See, in the car you asked about Jewish days being from evening to evening and Mari said that ‘High Sabbaths’ can be any day of the week.”

Chamberlain put her plate on the coffee table. “I remember.”

“Right. Well, that made me think about the thing that bothered me when I first read the verses.”

Mari bent one leg onto the sofa and faced him. “What thing?”

“The sixth and seventh verses. The ones about the women buying the spices and anointing Jesus’ body.”

“What about them?” Chamberlain inquired. “That was a normal burial practice and is just like the embalming we do today. Isn’t that right, Mari?”

Mari answered. “Mostly. The Jewish spices have more religious significance than modern embalming but the principle of preserving the body is the same.”

Scribe picked up his printout. “Let me read the verses to you and tell me if you hear anything strange.”

They both waited while he dramatically cleared his throat. He read the verses, emphasizing key words as he spoke:

Luke 23:55: ‘The women who had come with him from Galilee followed, and they saw the tomb and how his body was laid.

Mark 16:1: ‘***When the Sabbath was over***, Mary Magdalene, Mary the mother of James, and Salome ***bought spices*** so they might go and anoint him.

Luke 23:56: ‘Then they ***returned, and prepared spices*** and ointments. ***On the Sabbath day they rested*** according to the commandment.

When he finished, he again held the paper up to his lips and waited for the epiphany to beam from their eyes.

Scribe broke the silence. “So how could they buy spices after the Sabbath but go home and prepare spices before the Sabbath?”

Chamberlain protested. “But these verses are out of order. The one from the book of Mark is sandwiched between two adjacent verses from Luke.”

“True. But why would Rock do that unless he was trying to show us something that wasn’t apparent by the usual order?” Their silence encouraged Scribe to pursue his thought. “I knew something was wrong but I couldn’t figure it out until I got the strong urge to ask for your help.” He looked at Mari.

Mari pulled it in and followed, “The High Sabbath?”

“Exactly. That knowledge is so basic for you that it probably feels meaningless. But the beauty of all this is that each of us brings information and perspective at the right time to keep us moving forward. I’m starting to believe this synchronicity is around us all the time.”

Chamberlain interjected. “Scribe, are you saying there were two Sabbaths during the resurrection week?”

“That’s the only thing that makes these passages sensible. Either there were two Sabbaths during that week or one of the accounts is wrong; but the women cannot have bought spices both before *and* after the Sabbath...unless two Sabbaths occurred that week, with a day in between.

Mari interjected. “Is it not simpler to believe that one of the authors, Mark or Luke, got mixed up and reported the details incorrectly?”

“Nope”, Scribe responded, “because all four canonical Gospels talk about the ‘Day of Preparation’ and the ‘High Sabbath’. I checked when I found the verse numbers. The only variation in the story is in the book of John. Instead of the women, John writes that that Nicodemus and Joseph of Arimathea wrapped the body in spices before placing it in the tomb, but the special Sabbath is still mentioned."

Chamberlain pressed her temples. "But even though John doesn't acknowledge the women at the tomb, he does have them at the crucifixion and Mary Magdalene as the first witness to the resurrection."

Scribe curved his lips upward. "Correct."

Chamberlain rejoined. "Typical patriarchy. Everybody knows the women were there throughout the entire Passion event. Well, at least the other three writers told the truth about who really did the burial work."

Mari picked up with her previous thought. "Since all four Gospel authors speak of the 'High Sabbath', it is reasonable to conclude that there were two Sabbaths during that week."

Scribe grinned. "If we're right, then these two Sabbaths are a map that will lead us to the actual days of Jesus' crucifixion and resurrection."

Chamberlain exhaled and raised her hands in front of her face. "Honestly Scribe, who cares what day Jesus died or rose from the dead? The only thing that matters for most people is that it happened, period. Why does it matter *when* it happened?"

Before Scribe could speak, Mari charged in. "It matters to me because Holy days divide more people than they unite. Inside religions, special days remind us of our journey with God. But we have also used these days to separate ourselves from the rest of humanity."

"Well said", Scribe nodded. "It's true. Religions use days to stake out identity and territory. It is commonly known by scholars that Constantine the Great created a national Sunday Law in year 321 to strengthen his disintegrating empire. Many people in Rome worshipped the sun as part of a nature religion. Later, some early Christians declared Sunday the Christian Sabbath based on the resurrection story. So as a savvy politician, Constantine seized the opportunity to unite the people by overlapping their beliefs and centering them around one common day of worship. So the 'S-O-N' Day for Christians was merged with the 'S-U-N' Day for Pagans to become 'Sunday' for everyone in the new, Holy Roman Empire."

Mari grimaced. "That didn't work out too well for Jews."

Scribe admitted, "Unfortunately, you're right. This combining of the Roman Empire around a sanctified Sunday distanced Christianity from Judaism and deteriorated Jewish-Christian relations; which arguably fueled much of the world's anti-Semitism and Jewish genocide."

A light bulb came on for Mari. "But if Sunday wasn't the Resurrection day, then there's a new story to tell with new possibilities for us all."

Chamberlain squinted and frowned, looking away from Mari. "So Scribe, what day do *you* think he got up?"

FORTY

Rabbi Mizrah stormed into his office and slammed the door. The thick, Mediterranean Pine barrier was built more for privacy than beauty. All the furnishings had their own story buried deep below multiple layers of dust.

His operatives on the police force had informed him of two rabbis seen leaving Zamalek Residence around midnight. Mizrah knew all the Hebrew clergy in the city and none fit the description of these two. However, the sketch he held in his hand resembled two newcomers he'd encountered earlier in the evening.

Seeing her with Zogby triggered the memory of how Mari's father had brought an outsider wife into their midst along with their half-breed child. The wife tried to blend in, but Mizrah noticed the child had confrontation in her eyes from the moment she set foot inside the Synagogue. One day Mizrah had her cornered in the garden and planned to teach her a lesson when Zogby appeared with his arms folded. His wordless stare and outstretched hand beckoning for Mari warned Mizrah that she was off limits and not to be bothered in any way.

Afterwards, anytime Mizrah saw Mari, Zogby always stood within earshot; sweeping or mopping or something. Zogby never shirked his duties so there were no grounds to fire him. Besides, he had credibility with the older congregants and Mizrah could lose his position in the rabbinical order if the Mari episode ever came out. So he'd decided to wait. But he didn't have to wait long because, soon after, Mari's family left the community and her burning stares with them. But he never forgot her piercing glare and could see it even in the rude sketch of the shorter rabbi.

On Mizrah's orders, Rockman's apartment had been thoroughly searched, yielding a white Styrofoam head and strands of a sheitel scattered over the dresser and floor. Mizrah pounded on his desk when he deduced why Rockman needed a religious wig worn by married Jewish women in his bedroom. He picked up the phone and dialed, wiggling his knee harder with each ring.

Knock, knock, knock! Everyone turned toward the door with nowhere to hide except inside the two-person Jacuzzi. They remained perfectly still, trying to suppress the reflex to run but knowing their only option was to wait.

The second time the visitor rapped louder and faster. "Scribe, it's Jack. Open up."

When Scribe got Jack's earlier text, he replied with Chamberlain's suite number as the meeting place. Chamberlain placed her hand on her chest and exhaled. Scribe bustled toward the peephole and turned the handle.

Jack stood there frozen with no smile. Scribe thought nothing of it given Cocoa's kidnapping and the fact that it was four in the morning. But Jack had been instructed on the ride over to act normal or he'd be the cause of someone getting hurt. Scribe too felt the lateness of the hour, until he began walking backwards, strangely retreating while Jack advanced. Within a few steps Chamberlain could see the revolver sighted on Scribe's nose and his hands rise into the air.

Jack apologized but Scribe only half heard him. He was preoccupied trying to both anticipate and dodge a bullet from point blank range. So far, no strategy had come to him.

"You are a very elusive man", Wahid said with a straight face. "Without Jack, it would have taken me much longer to find you."

"David, keep walking", a voice from behind him commanded. Wahid's expression intensified when he saw the pistol Mari had aimed at his forehead. He knew there was no chance she would miss from this range so he was forced to let this Mexican standoff play itself out.

Wahid held his weapon trained on Scribe while sneering at Mari. "I never pegged you as a killer, Mari, but anything is possible." Wahid made sure that Jack stayed positioned between her and himself to discourage a surprise kill shot. He kept his hand on Jack's left shoulder, scouting the premises.

Scribe sniped. "The way I figure it, you're the killer Wahid."

The statement brought Wahid's eyes back to Scribe. "How's that?" Wahid scoffed and dared Scribe to answer.

"You're the only other person who has access to the information we found today. You knew Rock was here in Cairo and that he taught at the University. You had us tailed and you could have known about Adeena and the apartment. For all we know, you could've had Saba tail us and then thrown him off the roof at St. George's because he wouldn't help you murder us like you murdered Rock." Scribe's nostrils flared and his fists clenched.

Wahid raised his gun slightly. "Right. I sent my best man to follow you and then followed him before killing him? Brilliant. I am sure the magistrates will enjoy your American fairytale. It seems to me that you are the one who left a trail of dead bodies everywhere you visited today. I don't know how you faked your arrival records, but believe me, I will find out and you will stand trial for all three murders."

Scribe set his jaw line. "What about the beads you hid from us?" Wahid looked stunned and Scribe continued feeling empowered. "Don't play dumb. The beads you found in Rock's hand after he died?" Scribe protruded his neck and stretched his eyes into a question. "You told us it was a shadow."

Wahid flickered his gaze to Mari and registered agreement in her expression. "I couldn't tell you everything. That was the biggest clue I had."

Scribe inched closer, "You mean the biggest clue you sat on. You never intended to go public with those beads because you were protecting the fact that one of your sect might be the killer." Everyone in the room looked puzzled except Scribe and Wahid. "Why don't you tell everybody what 'C.O.S.M.' stands for?"

Wahid looked like a six year old caught with fire alarm ink on his hands. Scribe inched a micro step closer, searching for the right moment. His words were patronizing and intentional. "Let me help you out: 'Church…Of…Saint…Mark', which is a lesser known name for the Coptic Church."

Chamberlain choked back tears. "Scribe, you think the police are helping the man that killed my Matthew?" She stood, cheeks quivering, hate willing her tears away. "No. Did this man kill Matthew?

Scribe kept his focus on the gun barrel aimed at him. "I don't know if he did it or if he knows who did it, but he's definitely covering up the fact that the killer could be a Copt." Scribe prepared to pounce when Wahid finally spoke.

"Don't do it or I will be forced to shoot my way out of here." With the speed of the Waco Kid, Wahid pulled another pistol from his side waistband and swept across the torsos of all present. "Everyone, please be seated."

Reluctantly, Scribe took a seat near Mari, however Mari never faltered in her stance or in keeping her gun trained on Wahid.

"Mari, do not push me." His voice was gruff and grave as he aimed the revolver at her chest.

"Lamir", Mari stepped forward, "you know me and you know I would not help anyone guilty of murder." Wahid ground his teeth while Mari continued. "I also know that you had nothing to do with this. So we need to work together to figure things out and find Cocoa before it is too late."

Scribe blurted, "Why did he hide the beads from us?"

Mari's blank expression faced Wahid. He softened as the words flowed. "My family was almost killed in a police raid last year. The government is constantly looking for an excuse to order a wholesale assault on my people. I didn't know if a Copt was actually responsible for the murder of Rabbi Rockman, but I knew that the entire Coptic Church would be blamed if those beads were made public..." Wahid's eyes moistened. "...and I couldn't allow another massacre to happen."

Scribe understood prejudice. The American South was littered with cases of 'discretionary' arrests and shootings by police on unarmed minorities. Discrimination was a worldwide epidemic, so it wasn't hard for Scribe to believe that religious minorities in Egypt were susceptible to it as well.

Scribe followed up. "Okay, I can see that. But Mari, how can you be so sure he's not involved at all?"

She gripped her firearm with both hands. "Because, besides

being the most stubborn and pigheaded jerk on the Cairo Police Force, he's also the one with the most integrity. When I got passed over for his job, he was going to go to the Chief and insist that I be promoted instead. But I told him we would both be fired if he did that and somebody needed to remain and keep things honest." A twinkle appeared in her eyes. "Also, I have a strong feeling that we need him with us to make things right."

Wahid felt perspiration on his mustache and lowered his gun as Mari lowered hers. "Okay, talk."

FORTY ONE

Mizrah contemplated his answer before speaking. "Where is the girl now?"

The person on the other end of the telephone responded, then Mizrah resumed. "It had to be done. Leverage. Yes, I know. Rockman? They what? The team told me they found sheitel hairs strewn everywhere. He was planning to smuggle that girl out of the country. Exactly. I knew he was trouble the first time I laid eyes on him. I should have guessed then that he could destroy everything. Sure. Of course. Saba was unfortunate but what's done is done. I'll call you when I get there."

Mizrah depressed the button, pausing before placing the receiver back into its cradle. Things were getting hairier by the minute, but he couldn't afford for things to get out of hand or for any of this to trace back to him.

He hit the intercom and commanded, "Ephraim, come."

Five seconds later the heavy door swung on its hinges and Ephraim rushed in eagerly awaiting instructions. He'd been the Rabbi's assistant for eighteen months but had been a member of the Synagogue his whole life. Ephraim's family took pride at his being chosen to assist in God's work and Ephraim had great personal respect for Mizrah, both as a Rabbi and as a man. He felt especially honored to provide service to the community when so many were unable or unwilling.

"Yes Rabboni?" Close followers often called their rabbis 'Rabboni' as a term of endearment. Ephraim was about as close as followes got.

Mizrah waved him in. "Sit down. I want to ask you something."

Ephraim sat in a locally crafted, lacquered chair positioned to the left of the door.

Mizrah came around to the front of his desk and propped himself against the edge. "Do you remember those two visitors we had during Shabbat service?"

Ephraim nodded.

"Have you ever seen them before?"

Ephraim shook his head. "No Rabbi. I did feel like I knew the woman from somewhere, but I could not determine if it was so. After the cyclist fell, I stopped concentrating on the matter."

"Of course. Well, the man was a friend of Rabbi Rockman and the woman was briefly a member of our community many years ago."

Ephraim leaned in. "Who is she?"

"Her name is Mari. It's been almost thirty years since she's been here." Ephraim looked up and to the left, accessing memories that had long ago been filed away. He recalled a dark-haired little girl with unmistakable eyes that had stolen his heart when he was a young boy. He doubted if she even knew he existed since they had never actually spoken and he was two years younger than she.

Ephraim recovered. "Why did they come?"

"Good question", Mizrah snorted. "They were spotted impersonating rabbis near the scene of a murder at the American University and leaving Rabbi Rockman's secret apartment."

Murder? Secret apartment? It was a lot for Ephraim to take in. He'd liked Rabbi Rockman and he definitely liked Mari. But when Mizrah forbade Rockman to return to the Synagogue, Ephraim trusted that it was for the good of the community. Mizrah's story and tone seemed to demand that Ephraim turn his back on Mari, too. This would be more difficult since she had lived in his imagination as the perfect woman all these years.

Ephraim fired off three questions in rapid succession. "What is their connection to Rabbi Rockman? Do you think they killed him? Did they come to harm you? I won't let anything happen to you, Rabboni." Ephraim stood.

Mizrah motioned for him to sit. "I know, Ephraim. I know. I have known you since birth and picked you for an appointed time because I see myself in you. Like you, my work has been done for the good of the Jewish Faith. Though you obeyed, I know you questioned my judgment with Rabbi Rockman."

Ephraim protested. "No Rabbi. It was…"

Mizrah held up his hand gently. "There is no need. Everyone was clearly fond of him, including you. He did have a charming way. But charm is the cousin of deceit. To me, he did not have the best interest of the community at heart. He cared more for a dead Jesus than any of us put together. That bothered me."

Ephraim spoke before he realized. "But Rabbi, Jesus was a Jew. He was one of us."

Mizrah repositioned himself, sliding down the edge of the desk toward Ephraim. "Though Jesus was one of us, he did not honor our customs and, in death, he fueled the hatred and bigotry of our enemies. His words were used to diminish the authority of Judaism and his followers treated persecuting Jews as an act of devotion to him. Now the Torah is treated as a mere precursor to his words, which are nothing but regurgitated phrases from the Law and the Prophets."

"I agree, Rabbi. But it appears that the blame lies with Christians and not with Jesus."

"Yes Ephraim, but they speak for him and put words in his mouth that make us sound backwards and primitive. This is why I deemed Rabbi Rockman's obsession with Jesus unhealthy for us. His death was untimely but Yahweh sometimes works in mysterious ways."

Ephraim cringed inside, confused on how to interpret Mizrah's last statement. "Do you think Yahweh would will Rabbi Rockman to be harmed?"

Mizrah shrugged. "I think that Yahweh would preserve us the way that He always has. I cannot say that Yahweh wills murder, but it is apparent from the Torah that He called our forefathers to kill the Canaanites and secure the Promised Land. It is understandable to have philosophical thoughts on these matters but, in all cases, blessed be the name of the Lord and His will must be done."

Gripping the arms of the chair Ephraim replied, "Yes Rabbi."

Mizrah changed his tone. "We can only pray that Mari and her friend were not involved in Rabbi Rockman's murder and the murder of a young Muslim woman he was…seeing."

Secret apartment? Secret girlfriend? This new information unsettled Ephraim. Love was no crime. But in a context where Judaism was under siege, fidelity for Islam was tantamount to betraying the faith. Ephraim stood and clutched his chest. "I will protect you, Rabboni."

Mizrah embraced him and opened the door. "Get some rest and enjoy the remainder of your Sabbath."

Watching until Ephraim rounded the corner, Mizrah closed the door and sauntered back to his desk. He slumped with his hands folded in his lap, contemplating the next move. This was all getting a bit messy and he had to figure out how to ease out of it in one piece. Reclining, he saw Ephraim's shawl lying across the armrest of the guest chair and smiled as he heard a knock at the door.

Mizrah cracked the door in a jovial tease. "I figured you'd need…". His voice trailed off when he recognized his interlocutor. Not the visitor he'd expected.

Mari and Scribe took turns bringing Wahid up to speed on the meaning of the verses. He'd glanced at them, but the police cryptographers were looking for a hidden code in the words and, as yet, had come up empty. Via Jack, Scribe and Mari knew they had to get to St. Sergius, but they couldn't go without the information for which Rockman had been killed.

Chamberlain repeated her previous question. "So what day did he get up?"

Scribe stood and paced the floor. "Okay. We know that Mary Magdalene came to the tomb before daybreak early Sunday morning and Jesus was already risen." They agreed. "We also know that the day after he died was a 'High Sabbath', there was a day in-between, and then the regular Friday evening to Saturday evening Sabbath occurred." They agreed again. "So let's start from the second Sabbath and work our way backwards."

Jack found his voice, which momentarily silenced everyone else. "If we need a 'High Sabbath' day and then a regular day before Friday evening, that's two days. Two days before Friday evening puts the crucifixion on a Wednesday. The story says Jesus hung from the sixth to the ninth hour. In our time that's noon to

3pm. There were only three hours left until the 'High Sabbath' began, which means his burial was probably a rush job. So I don't think there would've been time to put the spices on his body until afterwards."

Scribe was proud, but he didn't take the opportunity to beam. "Yeah, John's burial account seems unlikely. But if Jesus is in the grave before 6pm on Wednesday, then three whole days from then has him resurrecting on Saturday evening before 6pm. So Dr. Chamberlain, to answer your question, if the Bible gives an accurate account of Jesus' crucifixion, burial, and resurrection, then it looks like Jesus got up at the end of the Saturday Sabbath, just before 6pm."

The entire room fell silent. Everyone considered what was said and no objections surfaced.

Finally Chamberlain protested. "Wednesday crucifixion and Saturday resurrection? I don't know. Somehow 'Good Wednesday' doesn't have the same ring to it." Scribe and Jack laughed, thankful for the comic relief.

Wahid took the floor. "And the motive for Rockman's death is?"

Scribe answered. "He either stumbled across this info or figured it out on his own. Either way, somebody didn't want him telling anybody else and they killed him for it. The last event we know of before Rock's death was the email to me. That makes me think it was still fresh for him because he didn't tell me and he seemed in a hurry."

Wahid conceded the point. "But what does it matter when Jesus resurrected?"

"I hate to admit it but I agree with Wahid here", Chamberlain mumbled.

Scribe put on his professor voice. "Wahid, I imagine that part of what anchors your faith in Christian salvation is the fact that Jesus fulfilled all the prophecies written concerning him. Am I right?"

Wahid crossed his hands in front of him, still standing in the same spot. "That's correct."

"So if he said that something had to happen a certain way, could the thing happen in a way other than what he said?"

Wahid grimaced. "Like what?"

Scribe pointed to the desk in the corner. "Get that Bible and read Mark 8:31 aloud."

Wahid flipped the pages and cleared his throat. "Then he began to teach the twelve that the Son of Man must undergo great suffering, and be rejected by the elders, the chief priests, and the scribes, and be killed, and after three days rise again." He looked up at Scribe suspiciously.

"Now if any of those things didn't happen, then Jesus lied to his disciples, right?"

Wahid swallowed before forcing out a cautious, "Technically speaking, yes."

"Okay. Now would you agree that lying is a sin?"

Wahid relaxed and lowered the Bible. "Thou shall not bear false witness. Of course, lying is a sin."

"Good. Then it stands to reason that Jesus had to spend three whole days in the grave for his words to be true and for him to qualify as a sinless sacrifice, right?"

Wahid was stumped. He grilled suspects all day and knew how to banter back and forth with the best of them. But his faith was such a guarded aspect of his life that he'd not thought very much about the interior of it and certainly wasn't accustomed to discussing it with a room full of strangers. So he put his police officer face back on. "Conclusion?"

"The conclusion, Inspector, is that if Jesus was crucified on Friday or even Thursday afternoon, then there is no way he got up before sunrise on Sunday and stayed in that grave three whole days. If he didn't, then besides being a liar, the conditions for Christ to save humanity would not be met."

Wahid put his finger on his temple and closed his eyes. Scribe kept going.

"But the Wednesday crucifixion fulfills Jesus' self-prophecy and is supported by the Gospel accounts. Counting three days from Wednesday evening before 6pm means that Jesus rose on Saturday evening before 6pm. And a Sabbath resurrection opens the possibility that both Jews and Christians can share Jesus and his message. The Sabbath Day could reunite Jews and Christians around their common link: Jesus. Both groups could reach their spiritual potential together, instead of opposed to each other."

"Huh", Mari moaned. "If this is true, it would resolve a lot of contradictions."

Jack jerked his head. "Hey Prof., this Wednesday business sounds familiar. Did we cover something like this in a class or one of the readings?"

Scribe didn't cover anything like this in his seminars, but he'd learned in the past 24 hours to respect people's intuitions, no matter how offbeat they appeared at first. "I don't think so, but what comes to mind?"

Jack talked with his hands, extending his index and second finger like a boy scout, swirling them while making his point. "I remember some sort of old book that talked about Jesus eating the Passover with his boys before he got captured. Dida...Dida something?"

Scribe knitted his brow. The only person he'd ever spoken to about that book was Rockman. In fact, Rockman had been the one who told him about the book shortly after they started hanging out at Westerville. Rockman always threw factoids at Scribe to keep their Jesus conversation going. He'd given Scribe the history of the document and a sketch of its contents, but Scribe had dismissed it as another Shroud of Turin typed artifact, until now.

"The document is called the *Didascalia Apostolorum* and I don't know how on earth you know about it because I'm sure you've never seen it or even heard its name. It literally means 'Doctrine of the Apostles' and claims to have been written by the Twelve during the first-century Council of Jerusalem recorded in Acts 15. Many scholars date it to third century Syria, but it's said to contain details that suggest the writers were eyewitnesses to the Last Supper and the arrest of Jesus before his crucifixion."

Scribe took a sip of water. "I can't believe we're even talking about this or that I remember as much as I do. Anyway, most of the *Didascalia* is about practices and the different clergy offices in the Church. But it is believed to contain an account of Passion Week that has Christ eating the Passover with his disciples on Tuesday. I remember it exactly as Rock recited the passage to me: 'For when we had eaten the Passover on the third day of the week at even, we went forth to the Mount of Olives; and in the night they seized our Lord Jesus'."

Mari wandered into Scribe's reasoning. "The third day is Tuesday, which would put the crucifixion on..."

Scribe nodded his head. "Um humph...on Wednesday." He could hardly believe it as the words rolled off his tongue. It wasn't the words as much as the setting and conversation that produced them.

Chamberlain's statement-question echoed. "So this *Didascalia* would back up your whole theory?"

"It looks that way." Scribe gave her a tired smile and she reciprocated.

Mari's head swam with all the information flying through the air. "So where is the document?"

Such a simple question. So simple that it tore through Scribe's mind like a runaway twister. *The Document? The Document.* "Oh my God, The Document!" Scribe shouted, startling everyone in the suite. "The email said, 'I Found It'. Don't you see, Mari? Rock found the Document. He found the *Didascalia Apostolorum*!"

Scribe figured Mari's muted reaction was a loss for words given the magnitude of his epiphany. But her blank stare meant her focus wasn't on the gravity of his discovery.

All eyes except Scribe's homed in on the doorway. Partially hurt, Mari choked back disbelief while staring down the barrel of the two loaded guns Wahid had unholstered and drawn like Billy the Kid. He could kill her and Scribe in the same motion, and she knew it. She had better aim, but Wahid could get off two rounds for every shot she took. Before she could finish her thought or Scribe could object, Wahid hissed, "This has been fun. Now Mari, drop your weapon and kick it over to me."

FORTY TWO

The van pulled to a halt on a gravelly road in a deserted section of Old Cairo. The side panel swung open and Cocoa was hoisted into the air like a mummified sack of potatoes. Her first though was to kick and struggle but, after looking down from almost seven feet in the air, she decided against getting dropped headfirst on the dark concrete.

"Patience child. This will all end when your friends do what I have asked."

Cocoa tried looking around to remember a marker or leave a trail, but she couldn't see a thing. And it seemed like the more he walked, the darker it got. It was as if she were descending into Plato's cave or worse: Dante's Inferno. The pungent odor smelled of mildewed stone and caused Cocoa to involuntarily gag.

"You Americans know nothing of sacrifice. We, on the other hand, we know much. For I reckon that the sufferings of this present world…". The Keeper quoted a verse from the book of Romans. Even though St. Mark was their namesake Apostle, St. Paul had always been his personal favorite. Paul's singular example of self-denial for the faith was unparalleled by any of the Twelve. The Keeper identified himself as a Paul amongst his brethren.

"It will not be long now until this all comes to an end. The only fight worth fighting is the good fight. And it will be won at all costs."

Cocoa heard every word, and prayed silently that she would wake up from this nightmare sooner than later.

The handcuffs securing Scribe and Mari grew tighter with every twist and wriggle. Wahid ordered Mari to place the restraints onto Scribe before he had Jack return the favor on her. He stationed another guard outside the suite door with authorization to shoot Jack if he tried to escape. Indo had to be sent home since he hadn't quite recovered from his earlier ordeal. So, once again, Jack found himself a prisoner, just with a different cellmate.

Chamberlain protested citing her social importance, yet when Wahid threatened her with an after-the-fact accessory to murder charge, her resolve weakened as her worries about being treated with dignity suddenly faded.

With Wahid shoving them every five feet, Scribe and Mari stumbled down the corridor, looking back in disgust but not having many options for retaliation; especially considering the two goons posted at the elevator.

Mari took the risk. "I trusted you, Lamir. How could you?"

Wahid holstered his revolvers. "How could I what? You expect me to let the prime suspects roam free because I know one of them personally? Mari, you know me better than that. I'm all about the job."

She countered. "Is your job to let innocent young girls die? Because this will happen if you keep us from going to St. Sergius. If anything happens to Cocoa, her blood is on your hands."

Scribe gave him a steely glare. "And if that happens, your blood will be on my hands."

One of the bodybuilders moonlighting as a cop gave Scribe a punch in the ear that sent him down on two knees. The ringing made him feel like Big Ben had crept up behind him and started chiming.

"That's all you got?" Scribe strained to stand while wincing, unable to cover his aching ear.

Wahid shook his head and exhaled. "No it's not. He'll have a buffet of pain waiting for you when we get back to the station."

The elevator arrived and Scribe managed not to get any more bruises before it reached the ground floor. Wahid had them placed in the backseat of his vehicle, still restrained. He turned the rear heat on to soften their resistance. It occurred to Scribe that the only good thing about his predicament was that he didn't have to smell the exhaust from junky pickup trucks in the wee hours. The night would soon blend into morning but the city was not yet awake. The early merchant traffic merely put Cairo in the first stages of stretching and yawning.

Mari shouted, even though Wahid could hear her if she whispered. "Lamir, how could you kill Saba? He was the best friend you had on the force."

Wahid screeched on the brakes and flipped the cruiser into park from the steering column. "You think I…? How dare you?" He gritted his teeth and cleared his throat. "Okay, you want to know how I know your boyfriend killed Rockman?" Wahid was breaking his usual methods of not revealing his hand with suspects until the case was ironclad: "The phone call."

Mari knitted her brow, lashes almost touching Wahid's seatback. "What phone call?"

Wahid jumped up and down in the seat motioning with both hands. "Ask him about the call he made to Rabbi Rockman the night of the murder."

Scribe had an irritated, puzzled grimace when Mari posed the question with her expression. He swiveled from Mari to Wahid. "Dude, what are you talking about?"

Wahid put his back on the steering wheel and focused on Scribe.

"In Rockman's email, he said he had to end the communication because his phone was beeping." Wahid paused to let his statement soak in. "Imagine my surprise when I checked his phone records and the call that came in registered your mobile number." Wahid held up a sheet of paper with a list of incoming and outgoing calls. At the bottom of the list, a number was highlighted at 11:57pm on the night Rockman was murdered. The dazed expression on Scribe's face told Mari that he didn't know how to address Wahid's accusation.

Wahid closed the latch on his trap, turning to Mari with a stone jaw line. "Mari, I swear, friend or no, I will make sure you get life in prison for helping this murderer go on his killing spree. First he kills his own friend, then he kills Saba and the girl to cover it up. I don't know how, but somehow, you helped him and I'm going to prove it."

Wahid slapped the dashboard with the palm of his hand, reminding Scribe of when he got paddled in fifth grade for talking during the Pledge of Allegiance. He felt an imaginary twinge of pain in his right buttock.

Mari met Wahid's stare. "We already told you. The man in the black cloak killed Saba and Adeena…and probably Rabbi Rockman. I'm sure he's involved in Cocoa's kidnapping and we have to get to St. Sergius before he kills her, too."

She didn't blink and, after a long while, Wahid eventually looked away. If looks could kill, he'd have laser beam holes in his eye sockets. Wahid knew Mari and that look was her 'You'd better believe me or you'll be sorry' look. He'd seen it many times over the course of their interaction in the Department, but he'd never been on the wrong end of it before. He'd also never seen any challengers left standing after the dust cleared and the facts came out. Every time someone had ever doubted her word, they'd always eaten a bucket of crow in the end.

But she has to be involved, he voiced to himself. *I know they're in this together*. Wahid stared into his lap and after reading the contents of his phone, pounded his thighs, snatched the car into gear, and sped off.

"Mari" was the only word Scribe could get out before she stopped him. "I know, David. I know. That would mean that I helped you do it. Since I did not, there is no need to explain."

Scribe took miniscule comfort in her support. Considering their circumstances, miniscule might be the biggest slice of comfort he'd have for a long time. So he cherished it.

He touched her on the knee and replied. "Thanks." Shifting and leaning he said, "But who do you think used my phone to call Rock? I packed it in my luggage, so it was in Cairo on Wednesday but I didn't know Rock's Egyptian mobile phone number."

Mari pondered and whispered, "I collected your bag on Friday from unclaimed baggage about an hour before you arrived. If someone used your phone to call Rabbi Rockman, they had plenty of time to put it back before I retrieved the bag."

Scribe spoke emphatically. "But who knew I was coming? I barely knew 24 hours before the ticket was purchased."

"I don't know. But when we find out, we'll also find our killer."

Mari hadn't felt trapped like this since Mizrah encroached upon her in the courtyard garden. Zogby had been her guardian angel then. She sure could use him now to help her out of this one.

The fusion of subtle sunrays and moonlight that hazed the pre-dawn streets produced a foggy illumination that gave the arcane structures an eerie glow. The same Internet Café where it all began stood darkened in Wahid's rearview mirror. The drive may as well have been in a horse and buggy for all the turbulence they endured in the backseat. On those streets you had two choices: either drive like a tortoise and preserve your car for further voyages or drive like a hare and replace your undercarriage when the metal scraped off after hitting a cobblestone speed bump.

It was all Mari could do to keep from dry heaving. Her anxiety about lockup didn't help matters because she knew what happened to women in a cell. If they found out she was a former cop, whatever happened would happen sooner than later, and more painfully.

Mari closed her eyes to soothe the nightmare of prison, hoping she'd awaken when her eyes reopened.

Wahid stopped at a red light and put the car in park. Turning the last corner his phone scuttled onto the passenger floorboard and he reached across the seat to retrieve it. Once in hand, he righted himself and wrapped his palm around the gearshift when he felt a warm metal tube lodge into his ear and a slender arm snake around his headrest. Cradling his neck, Mari spoke firmly. "Lamir, do not make me shoot you. Do as I tell you."

"May I come in, Rabbi?" The Italian had a light way about him, suggesting the visitor thought very little of his host.

Mizrah pulled the door wider without words and walked

deliberately back to his seat. He placed his hairy forearms on the desk and watched the visitor pace forward. Mizrah was accustomed to one way communication from this man's employer, so he sat awaiting the purpose of the visit.

The visitor's tone was entreating, yet brimming with a passive ultimatum. "Rabbi, our friends in Rome are *uncomfortable* with the way the situation has been handled. They are looking for quick resolution and have asked me to come and impress this desire upon you."

Mizrah hated lawyers, but Vatican lawyers were the worst. He knew he had to control his contempt. He lifted his wrists and spoke reassuringly. "Padre, there was no need for you to come all this way. The situation is under control."

The visitor stroked his own neck, revealing a priest's collar nestled beneath his black trench coat. "Our intelligence reports slightly different information. Rabbi, need I remind you of the severity of this matter?"

Mizrah shook his head. The priest exhaled, then resumed. "We have protected your community as well as the Coptics from persecution for over a thousand years. It would be a shame if something were to happen to your families at this time. But if it does not serve our interests to expend the social capital, your fate is beyond my control. You understand our predicament, do you not?"

Mizrah nodded rapidly. "Yes, and I assure you that the Document has been secured and all exposed to it have been contained."

The priest picked up a cigar from Mizrah's desk and rubbed the length of it underneath his nose. "I trust for your sake that you are right." The priest replaced the cigar, retraced his steps, and left without another word.

FORTY THREE

The Kel-Tec P-32 lodged against Wahid's eardrum had a bluish tint covering its compact but deadly cavity. Affectionately called a mousegun, Mari concealed the semi-automatic pistol in the small of her back before leaving Rockman's apartment. It wasn't the strongest handgun on the market, but Wahid knew that at point blank range, the 9mm rounds could tear a hole in his head the size of a walnut. So he handed Mari his car and handcuff keys like she instructed.

Wahid kicked himself for not frisking her before putting them in the back. He remembered she always carried a second weapon while on the job, but all the excitement made him careless. It was little consolation that she was no longer a police officer because they'd heard countless times from retired detectives, "Once a cop, always a cop."

"David, unlock yourself and cuff Lamir to the steering wheel."

Scribe felt like an amateur in the presence of a seasoned professional. Mari never took her eyes off Wahid when she handed him the keys and Scribe didn't say a word. He wondered how in the world she'd removed her handcuffs but didn't ask out of awe and the sheer desire to obey her command.

After Wahid was secured, Mari slid out of the rear driver's side door and met Scribe near the front windshield.

"We're not taking the car?", Scribe questioned.

"No. The car has GPS tracking inside so the police could follow our every move. Plus, Lamir could get hurt out here in the streets of Old Cairo."

Wahid stared at the dashboard, avoiding eye contact.

Scribe protested. "Well, if we leave him in the car he could just lay on the horn until somebody comes and calls his buddies."

Mari chuckled. "This is true. But considering the number of people in this neighborhood he has personally arrested, I do not believe he would draw that kind of attention to himself."

Scribe jangled the car keys, smiling as they left Wahid parked in the predawn shadows. He pocketed the keys and turned to Mari. "Hey, how did you slip those handcuffs?"

She grinned. "Remind me to kiss Jack the next time I see him. He placed the setting on medium instead of small. When I started to perspire, my wrists and hands were sweaty enough to slide out with very little effort. I was surprised, too."

"Good ole' Jack." Scribe guffed. "So what's the plan?"

"I do not have one yet. But we cannot simply walk into St. Sergius without knowing what we are up against."

Scribe responded. "I agree. I recall Wahid saying something about 'the Keepers'. Who are they?"

Mari kept walking. "Until tonight, he and I both thought they were Coptic mythology; that is, until one tried to strangle me at the University." She massaged her neck with her left hand.

Scribe shortened his stride. "Hmmm. I have a hunch that all this is happening in conjunction with something I saw in the newspaper at the hotel."

"What?"

"I read that the Pope is scheduled to stop in Cairo next week on the first leg of a Mideast Goodwill Tour."

Mari nodded. "It's probably another publicity stunt. Egyptians do not have much faith in Crusaders." Mari shrugged her shoulders. "Let us walk around and think awhile. Walking helps me to figure things out."

Scribe reminisced. "Just like Rock." Then it hit him like a ton of bricks. Almost dragging Mari by her arm Scribe shouted, "The Internet Café!"

Waiting five minutes, Mizrah slinked down the corridor, through the courtyard, and out the back gate. He tiptoed along the outer sidewalk draped in a darkly hued swathe with only his head, neck, and pants bottom visible. He remembered a shortcut that would get him there in half the time of taking the traditional route. Mizrah held his head down, only looking up occasionally, and his torso bent slightly as he pounded the root-lifted pavement underneath. *This should have been finished days ago*, he fumed, yet he found himself more exposed to risk than before Rockman's death.

Mizrah had been promised that if he provided information leading to the retrieval of the Document, his worries about the safety of their Synagogue and community would be over. Protection was assured from all harassment when the Document again rested securely in the Keeper's lair.

When the Keeper made contact with Mizrah, it had surprised him because of the candor and frankness of the discussion. It also surprised him that though nothing incriminating was said, no disguise veiled the Keeper's face or obscured his identity. Mizrah thought back on it all while pummeling the Old Cairo alley underfoot.

"May I speak freely with you Rabbi?", the Keeper had said to Mizrah as they strolled along the banks of the Nile.

"Of course", Mizrah slowed his pace, wondering about the nature of the business to be disclosed.

"One of your people has taken something from my people and I need it back."

Mizrah waited a calculated four seconds and replied, "Hmmm. Who is it and what was taken?"

"A Document. A very important Document that must be returned immediately. As for who took it, his name is Matthew Rockman."

Mizrah's temples began to tighten. "I banished Rabbi Rockman from returning to us seven months ago. I have not seen him since."

The Keeper continued undeterred. "That may be. Still he wormed his way into our ranks and fooled the Elders…but not me. I know it was him."

Mizrah was intrigued and wanted more information. "So why should I help you? You people have been nothing but trouble to us?"

The Keeper turned to Mizrah and said evenly, "Because if you do not, life can get very difficult…for all of us. But in return for your assistance, I guarantee that your neighborhood will be under our personal protection as well as the Vatican's."

For Jews in Egypt, friends were hard to come by. So even if this relationship was only because of mutual interest, given who was asking, it would have to do. Mizrah inquired, "What do you need?"

The Keeper handed him a mobile phone. "You will receive a text message containing Rabbi Rockman's telephone number tonight on your phone. When this happens, use this phone to call the Rabbi and persuade him to come to the base of the stairs at St. George's Church."

Mizrah placed the phone into his jacket pocket. "What if he refuses?"

The Keeper straightened his tie, letting all emotion drain from his face like a Vulcan before replying, "For the sake of your people, he'd better not."

Mizrah sliced through the breezeless night trying to convince himself that he didn't actually know what awaited Rockman after that phone call. Still, no matter how hard he tried to drown it with rationale, he couldn't overrule the physical twinge of conscience in his chest. When he'd considered the welfare of his community and possibility that their children could grow up without the danger of mob violence threatening to snuff out their lives, the decision was easy. However, upon remembering his police source's description of the nature of Rockman's demise, Mizrah's gag reflex kicked in:

"Hello", Rockman answered on the fourth ring.

"Rabbi Rockman? This is Rabbi Mizrah. I apologize for the lateness of the hour, but I need to speak with you."

Rockman clicked the 'send' button on his email and queried the reason, "What about?"

"I can't speak of it directly over the phone, but it's something that needs your immediate attention."

Rockman hummed while thinking of an excuse. "It's kind of late Rabbi. Can this wait until tomorrow?"

Mizrah felt Rockman slipping away and heard the Keeper's threat echoing in his head. He had to act quickly. "Matthew, I know there have been harsh words between us. I feel terrible about it and wanted to mend the breach in the spirit of Passover. When I learned the subject of my call, I was initially upset, but realized that this was Yahweh's will for me to make things right."

Rockman sat consumed with curiosity. Never in a million years did he expect to hear an apology coming from the man who told him he wasn't fit to be a Jew.

Mizrah seized upon the silence. "I'll just come out and say it. I know you have a Muslim lady friend at the American University."

The wind momentarily left Rockman's lungs. He'd worked diligently to conceal his affection for Adeena and knew people were watching, even if they didn't understand what they were seeing. A gesture here or a giggle there would give them away. So they'd been careful to keep their interactions explainable by their professional relationship. So he thought. Breathlessly he managed, "How did you…?"

Mizrah countered mid-sentence. "You know I have to know what's happening in Cairo for the good of our people. But do not worry. I am calling as a friend." He let that word linger in the air before continuing. "The Torah encourages Rabbis to marry so, in that, I can say your courtship is honorable. But the reason for my call is that Ephraim and I saw her near the stairs at St. George's a few moments ago."

Rockman interrogated, concerned. "Why? What was she doing there?"

"I could not tell you. She seemed safe and happy, looking up at the stars and laughing the way that young girls in love laugh. I just thought I should call you because it is late and she is a young woman alone on the streets of Cairo past tourist hours."

Whatever his motive, Mizrah had a point. Rockman still wasn't clear on how Mizrah knew about Adeena, but he did. And since he was right about their relationship, he could be telling the truth about Adeena at St. George's. It was only a three minute walk from the Internet Café, if that. Rockman thanked Mizrah, hurried to pay his tab, and ran out the door toward the ancient church.

Bending a deserted corner, Mizrah admitted to himself that he suspected Rockman would be injured by his deceiving phone call. He knew Adeena's family had no telephone so Rockman could not verify her whereabouts. Mizrah couldn't be certain he would go to the church, but if Rockman was smitten like the reports described, he'd break records sprinting toward those steps. *What's done is done,* he kept repeating as a mental mantra. *What's done is done.*

FORTY FOUR

The drowsy attendant recoiled with a jolt when Mari and Scribe jogged through the door. Gaunt and ashen, he seemed of college age and probably spent most of his free time lying, arms prone, across the Café counter.

"May I help you?", he offered cautiously with a startled residue waning in his eyes.

Scribe spoke. "Yes. Were you here the night the Rabbi was killed near St. George's?"

The attendant gave Scribe the once over. "Sir, I already gave my statement to the police. I've been over it five times." The attendant pointed toward the door. "He sat at the first computer, paid, and ran out before he got his change. That's all I know."

Scribe reacted, waving extended fingers. "That's plenty. Thanks."

He rushed over to the terminal, motioning for Mari to have a seat next to him. She gave the attendant a comforting sigh of mutual confusion and complied with Scribe's wishes.

She spoke as he typed. "So what are we looking for?"

"I honestly don't know. But I felt that if we had the same computer Rock used to send the message, it would somehow lead us in the right direction."

"The computer?"

Scribe kept his eyes on the screen. He depressed the down arrow and the page scrolled until it hit the bottom. Scribe was a self-taught speed reader due to graduate school professors who each thought that assigning five chapters a week was going easy on their students. "Not just the computer. But connecting the dots on the Pope's visit, the *Didascalia*, and trying to figure out why Rock got mixed up in this."

"I see. So what do you have so far?"

Scribe leaned forward. "It says here that all original copies of the *Didascalia* are extinct, but the Vatican is rumored to have one in its vault. The scholarly consensus is that the Document was written by a Catholic Bishop in Roman Syria, but St. Epiphanius believed the Twelve Apostles wrote it."

Mari waited a beat before asking. "Who's that?"

"Actually he was a pretty nefarious character who went around having people killed; suppressing non-orthodox texts and Christian practices. He was like an early Deputy Inquisitor who could have you burned at the stake for carrying around letters from the wrong people. It says here that he kept a compendium of the heresies he stamped out and, ironically, his accounts are the only surviving evidence of many versions of Christianity he helped to destroy."

Mari nodded. "But how is he connected to the *Didascalia*?"

Scribe returned to the screen. "Well, it looks like one of the groups he attacked was called the Audians, who believed that God has a human form and that Jesus was crucified on the exact day of Passover."

"Okay. But I don't see how the *Didiscalia*, St. Epiphanius, or the Audians tie into your friend getting killed."

"That's the thing. I didn't either…", Scribe crinkled his mouth as if chewing an imaginary crumb in the corner, "…until I considered the Pope's visit. But let me finish with the Audians and Epiphanius."

He resumed. "Now, Epiphanius recorded in his book of heresies that he found a document among the Audians that he believed was written by the Twelve Apostles at the first Council of Jerusalem."

Mari's jaw went slack. "The *Didascalia*?"

"The one and only." Scribe let that sink in before adding, "And guess who has his own, personal Feast Day on the Coptic Orthodox Calendar?"

Mari was speechless, momentarily. "So David, a Catholic Inquisitor testified to the authenticity of the *Didascalia* and is venerated by the Coptic Church?"

"Exactly. What's more, Epiphanius grew up in Egypt and his book of heresies describes the Audians as accusing the Catholic Church of changing the day of the crucifixion from Wednesday to Friday in honor of Emperor Constantine's birthday."

Mari rubbed her hands on her thighs. "This is an extreme indictment. Why would the Catholic Church consent to an alteration of this magnitude on such a central feature of Christian faith?"

Scribe scratched his head. "I think about it like this. According to his book, the *Panarion*, Epiphanius admits in…", Scribe glanced back at the screen, "…Book III, Chapter 9 that the Church used to celebrate Jesus' crucifixion on Passover. But if you work for a group of people who will kill you if you don't condemn their enemies, then you make up reasons why their enemies are wrong; even when blame lies with your bosses."

"All for power?"

"Look Mari. If you're trying to build a Universal Church, you can't have viable competition. You certainly can't look like a stepchild of Judaism if you're going to rule the world. You've got to create enough theological and chronological difference between your tradition and everybody else's to justify yourself. So changing the date of the crucifixion from Wednesday to Friday allowed the Church Fathers to obtain the real prize." Scribe tilted his head and smiled slyly. "Which was?"

Mari peered into his eyes, pensively, with her chin held up. "… which was a Sunday Resurrection."

Scribe unleashed a hushed shrieked. "Precisely!" The attendant's headphones audibly projected music through the synthetic cushions, but he sensed the vibration of Scribe's nearby sonic boom. He looked up to inspect Scribe and Mari, then lowered his head and went back to his magazine.

Scribe spoke rapidly. "Epiphanius' book has recently been translated into English, which opens the Western Christian world to read this for themselves." He volleyed with the irony. "I'll bet good money that when Epiphanius wrote his *Panarion* he never thought it would eventually bolster any of the doctrines he tried to eradicate."

Mari challenged Scribe's roll with sport. "And the Pope?"

"I don't know if the Pope is directly involved. But somebody in the Vatican is. His visit hints at the connection he has with all this. I can't say he's personally responsible for Rock's death. Still, I feel certain that this all ties together with the Resurrection-Day shift."

Scribe spun on his stool and typed the words 'Pope' and 'Sunday' into the search engine. Waiting for the results he offered, "I have a hunch."

Mari logged onto the computer in front of her and began the same search.

After reading for a couple of minutes, Mari stopped to compare notes. "What did you find?"

Scribe ran his finger down the screen before answering. "I found out who the Pope was during Constantine's reign."

Mari made a 'spit-it-out' hand gesture.

Scribe relented. "Pope Sylvester I. But that's not all." Scribe scooted his stool closer. "It is well known that Sunday worship is a practice that can be defended as dating back to the New Testament. But I found Catholic and non-Catholic sources affirming that Pope Sylvester decreed the official change of the Christian Sabbath to Sunday in memory of the resurrection."

"Hmmm. So coupled with Constantine's fancy, Pope Sylvester honoring Sunday was a way for Rome and the Church to eat their cake and have it as well."

Scribe pointed at Mari, smiling. "What did you get?"

Mari placed one hand on the desk. "Guess who issued an Apostolic Letter declaring Sunday the new Sabbath?"

It was Scribe who now engaged in the miming game. Mari relieved his torment. "Pope John Paul II."

Scribe furrowed his brows. "Wow. What did he say?"

She glanced back to her screen. "It's printed here. He said in an Apostolic Letter dated May 31, 1998 that, 'Sunday should be the weekly day in which the Church celebrates the resurrection of Christ. In obedience to the Fourth Commandment, Sunday must be sanctified, above all, by participation in Holy Mass'."

Mari finished reading and peered into Scribe's blank expression. "Well?"

Scribe cleared his throat before uttering. "You've just put the final piece in place." He grabbed her hands and spoke slowly. "Apostolic Letters have been historically treated as Canon Law. There were lots of rules and decrees scattered across the Catholic world and Pope Pius X decided to have them all collected into one Code of Church Law. The last Pontiff under whom Canon Law was revised was John Paul II."

Scribe had that toothy professor's grin of anticipation, but the implications hadn't dawned on Mari yet.

Scribe plowed on, shaking her wrists. "Don't you see? The Pope *as* Pope is infallible and inerrant. If he decrees Sunday is the day of the resurrection, then, according to those doctrines and Canon Law, it has to be. So if someone says he's wrong...well, it's their word against his infallible, inerrant word. But if somebody finds a historical document written by the Twelve Apostles that proves that any Pope, Sylvester I or John Paul II, made a theological error...".

Mari finished his sentence. "...it would undermine Papal authority and ultimately the authority of the Catholic Church itself."

Scribe's expression became grave. "And that's worth killing for."

The phone they commandeered from Wahid signaled an incoming message that they both read with baited breath: "If Scribe and Mari are not here in five minutes, the girl dies!"

Seeing the door swing, the attendant snatched off his headphones and hurriedly dialed the Police to report a theft. When asked the item he replied, "Uh, twenty-two minutes of computer services rendered."

FORTY FIVE

The foggy morning air grew thicker but couldn't dull the connection with her internal GPS. Mari leaned over to Scribe as they strode, barely breathing hard. "We have to be careful. There are police and armed sentry in certain locations on the street."

Scribe nodded and admired the grace of Mari's movements as they gaited from side-street to alley. Sprinting uphill past the roundabout, Scribe watched the massive dome of St. George's Church disappear behind the ancient retainer wall built by the Romans and supporting the staircase where Rockman was first attacked. Death seemed to be in the air, and they were running toward it full speed.

Reaching the corner of Rue St. Sergius, Mari and Scribe almost fell backwards when they say a bloody wristed man emerge from a nook, pointing a .44 caliber Colt Dragoon revolver at Scribe's cheekbone. Mari knew the gun because the precinct chipped in on it as a gift when he was promoted to Inspector. Wahid was an avid collector and obviously kept his prize possessions closer than home.

"Surprised Mari? Don't be. You're not the only one that can escape handcuffs." Wahid breathed in the satisfaction and continued. "The trick is to expand the bones in your hand while you're being cuffed. That way, they seem tighter than they are. Then you put your wrists together, line up your thumb and pinky with the rest of your hand, and yank like Hell until you tear your skin off." Wahid gritted his teeth as he chuckled, signaling that the ordeal was more painful than his ego would acknowledge.

"There *is* one thing that doesn't add up?" The unspoken 'What is that?' question hung in the air. Mari didn't know what to think and Scribe was praying that Wahid's concealing of the beads didn't include murdering them and dumping their bodies to hide the Coptic connection.

Wahid pulled out another collector's pistol and scratched his head with the barrel. "How did you know about the Document?"

Scribe tensed and willed himself to answer by blocking out the gunfire in his mind. "I told you, in conversation a few years ago." Scribe tried not to sound angry or unsure, and wondered if he'd done both instead.

Wahid scratched his stubble with the second gun and put it back into his jacket. "My grandfather told me bedtime stories about a secret Document that kept Coptics safe from harm and was guarded by a select group of priests called Keepers. He said these priests wore long, black cloaks and were sworn to protect the Document with their lives. This killer you described sounded outlandish until you mentioned the book. That brought a clarity to my mind like I haven't experienced since listening to my grandfather's stories as a child."

Scribe wanted to ask, "So you're not going to kill us?", but refrained.

Wahid resumed. "I tried to fight it. The case against you makes sense to me, so I acted on that by arresting you and driving you to the precinct. I felt normal again and focused on what the facts tell me is true. But when I'd just yanked off the cuffs and stopped the bleeding, I heard the dispatch call about the Internet Café and knew exactly where you two would be. Now if you'd killed the Rabbi and his girlfriend, why would you come here instead of escaping?"

Mari blurted. "That's what I've…". Wahid shifted the pistol in her direction and her voice trailed.

He studied them both before speaking again. "So your showing up here actually bought you the benefit of the doubt in my mind."

Wahid lowered the revolver. "From the stories I've heard, if the Keepers have your student, you're going to need more than guns when you ask for her back."

Mari and Scribe nodded their heads in silence at the tentative truce. "But make no mistake. If I find out that you really are the murderer, you're going down hard."

"Agreed." Scribe met Wahid's stare as a show of sober honesty. He also met the familiarity of Wahid's pistol aimed at his stomach.

Wahid motioned for them to start down the sidewalk and prodded Mari to lead the way. A lumbering man draped in a dark cloth had watched and heard the exchange between Wahid and Scribe. He kept his distance but followed them toward the doors of the most sacred Coptic Church in Egypt.

St. Sergius draws its name from Sergius of Rome, a soldier-saint martyred in the fourth century. The locals call it Abu Serga and affirm it as the oldest church in Cairo. But the worldwide claim to fame for St. Sergius is the belief that it covers the spot where the Holy family rested for thirty days after arriving in Egypt. Built in a Constantinople Basilica style, the church features two aisles and a tripartite sanctuary supported by four pillars. Yet none of them got the chance to see it, because the substantial double doors were dead bolted from the inside.

Scribe yanked on the impassible barriers, shaking the vertical handles. "No dice. What do we do now? We've got to get inside fast."

At the corner of the building stood a hooded giant. He looked like two people stuffed into one hammock and his face sank beneath the frock shrouding his head. He made no sounds, but his presence screamed fight or flight to anyone in his vicinity. When he was sure the trio noticed him, he turned and disappeared around the left side of the building.

"Hey!", Mari shouted. "Where's Cocoa?"

Scribe addressed the question in Mari's eyes. "We have no choice."

The three broke into a light sprint with Wahid cautiously bringing up the rear. He'd heard tales of Keepers having superhuman strength and powers granted to them by God for their special mission. And even though he had the gun, the guy he just saw looked like he could absorb every round in his clip and stay on his feet. What's more is that all Keepers are Coptics, and Wahid's personal mission was to protect his people from police assassination, not contribute to it.

Rounding St. Sergius, they witnessed the figure casually descend a short flight of steps and disappear into the side of the church.

"Where'd he go?", Scribe asked.

"It looks like he went into the crypt", Wahid added.

Mari automatically went into tour guide mode. "The crypt contains the remnants of the area where the Holy family is said to have hidden from Herod the Great. Much of it had succumbed to a fire in the eighth century. This is the only original portion that survives."

Scribe heard sloshing. "What's that?"

Mari answered. "No one has been inside the crypt for ages because it floods. Its subterranean location is susceptible to the rising Nile. I do not know what he's doing, but that crypt is full of water."

Wahid concurred. "Indeed. In fact, that crypt is ten feet deep so he is either swimming or drowning as we speak."

Scribe squinted. "But he was so nonchalant. He almost sauntered into that crypt like he was waiting on us to follow him. We've got to check it out."

Their collective inching toward the opening was interrupted by a woman's shrill cry. "Help. I'm in *here*."

"Cocoa?", Scribe and Mari called back in unison.

The voice responded. "Down here. Hurry!"

Taking the stairs in two strides, Scribe ventured into the crypt and came upon another set of descending steps surrounded by vertical wooden balusters on three sides. It gave the impression of an elevated cave of water waiting to drown all unwelcome wanderers. But if Cocoa was in there, Scribe couldn't live with himself unless he risked it.

Surprisingly, the water came just above the knees and the three navigated their wading with little difficulty. They all pulled out their phones to light the dark path and continued down the mouth of the crypt. The wall facing them contained wooden panels depicting the Nativity scene and Joseph working at the fortress to build the outer wall they had passed on the way. The panels were remarkably well-preserved considering the damp conditions in which they were kept.

"Is that a light near the wall?" Scribe saw flickering with the character of an oil lamp.

Mari responded. "Yes. But what is the image near the flame's shadow?"

Scribe peered, swooshing toward the painting and stopped. "It's Jesus with outstretched hands in front of the Pyramids." Looking to Mari, "Gloria told me she saw Rock standing in this position holding a scroll. This has got to be where he wanted me to go."

As they approached the south wall, a corridor emerged sealed by a waist-high barrier that dammed the water from proceeding any farther. Wahid felt like Noah when he finally found dry land. Soggy pants and all, the three scaled the synthetic dam. They immediately recognized the young woman tied to a chair and gagged between two burning lanterns posted on opposite walls. Cocoa had mixed emotions in her eyes when the group came into full view.

The Keeper stood poised behind her with another intricate dagger near her jugular vein. He hadn't planned to receive so many guests, yet accepted the task that fell to his hands to perform. Cocoa's positioning solidified the Keeper's advantage. She acted as a human shield against all types of ammunition. Perhaps he wasn't immortal, but he was meticulous.

He spoke deliberately. "I only expected two, but all things work together for the good. Wahid, thank you for making sure everyone arrived safely. Now Inspector, carefully place your gun on the ground and kick it to me." The Keeper brandished the blade in a cutting motion near Cocoa's esophagus.

Wahid knew that voice but he couldn't place it. There was no time to flip through his mental rolodex so he did as the voice commanded. The Keeper knelt to retrieve the weapon, placing it into his outer pocket. "You have been worthy adversaries, unlike your Rabbi friend."

Scribe clenched his fists on reflex without forethought. "Careful Professor. Wouldn't want to be hasty in the present situation. Things could get…messy." No sinister laugh accompanied this statement, escalating it in gravity.

Wahid had almost pinpointed the voice but it was somehow deeper and thicker than his subconscious remembered. Was it altered now or had it been altered the other times he heard it? The answer teetered at the edge of his mind just as the Keeper grabbed the front of his hood and peeled it back. Scribe had no reaction to what he saw. But Wahid's eyes widened and Mari's nostrils flared; both of their heartbeats quickened and their pulses raced like horses in the Kentucky Derby. In one motion, the nightmares of their childhoods and adult lives had meshed into one horrifying personification. Mari gasped. Wahid almost fainted from the amount of oxygen he inhaled when he saw the toothy grin of Chief Habash staring him in the face with a deep gash above his right ear.

FORTY SIX

On Holy Thursday, Egyptian Copts have a custom of praying in seven Coptic Churches after Mass to commemorate the Last Supper. If Habash was a Keeper, that meant he was also a Copt and had attended Mass and prayed a few hours after he murdered Rockman in cold blood.

Wahid started, stopped, and started again. "Sir, what are you doing here?" And then added, "What are you doing?"

Habash smirked. "Don't look so shocked. You know the legend, so you know what I am and why I'm here. You also know that I'm not alone."

Out of the shadows came twelve cloaked Keepers, none as big as Habash, but they each had ten inch blades held upright in their left hand like burning candles. Three of them stood an arm length away from the group so there appeared to be no chance of escape.

Sensing this, Scribe saw their best bet as trying to get Mari and Cocoa out while he and Wahid sacrificed themselves. "Cocoa, are you alright?" She nodded and moaned through the gag in her mouth and the blindfold she wore. Scribe continued. "Let her go. She's got nothing to do with this."

Habash scoffed. "True. She doesn't know who I am, but she could figure it out if I..." He snatched Cocoa's blindfold and craned his neck to face her. "Oh, well. Now she's seen my face. What a shame."

Multiple layers of revenge gurgled in Cocoa's throat as she spat, catching Habash in the pupil of his right eye. He bellowed, thrashing and rubbing his slimy eyeball with the base of his hand. In the process, Cocoa's chair tipped onto its side and Scribe rushed forward to untie her. The Keepers did not flinch as this occurred, obviously secure in the fact of their dominance and tactical advantage.

"You will regret that." Habash squeezed the handle of the dagger so tightly it almost vanished within his mammoth palm.

Huddled next to the others, Cocoa couldn't resist. "That's payback for tying me up and manhandling me chump. You're sick."

Wahid knew that in order for them to stay alive, he had to keep Habash talking. "Chief, why did you kill Rabbi Rockman?"

"Because he betrayed us. I was against making him one of us from the beginning, but he manifested the three-day Resurrection truth and could not be denied entrance."

"Rockman was a Keeper?" Wahid asked as if questioning his own question.

"Yes, for twenty four hours before his treachery was discovered and balance restored back to our Order."

The small, blue crucifix became visible when Habash performed a circular, cutting motion and made Scribe realize what happened to Rockman's wrist. He yelled at Habash, pointing and bending at the waist. "You're a liar. You killed Rock because he wasn't like you and you hated the fact that he knew your Jesus secret."

Habash glanced over at one of the Keepers, then back at Scribe. "The Rabbi said you were resourceful in his diary. I presume you deciphered the timeline with the clues he provided?"

Scribe's non-response told him the answer.

"Too bad you didn't do it under different circumstances. We would have invited you into the Order."

Scribe scowled. "No thanks. You guys killed Rock, and *he* was a member."

Habash stomped the chair Cocoa had been strapped to, crushing the legs. "He was never one of us. He infiltrated our ranks and stole the only thing that keeps the Coptic community protected from annihilation."

"The *Didascalia Apostolorum*?"

Habash jerked. "How do you know of it? The Rabbi said nothing in his correspondence with you."

"Not then, but we talked about it years ago." Scribe hadn't found a portal of attack just yet. He had to keep going. "Why would the Document protect you from annihilation?"

Habash grunted. "I grow impatient with your questions. Still, because you know of the book, you deserve satisfaction before your death." He scanned the circle of Keepers and resumed. "There are powerful people who have invested much into shaping the world into what we see. Religions fight each other because these people say there can be no peace."

He held up a clay-colored parchment bound with hemp in his hand. "This book contains information that would change that. Your friend stole it after his initiation, while we slept. He figured no one would immediately detect his deceit since the golden chest is only opened during inductions. His was the first in twenty-three years. I never trusted him, so I checked."

Scribe felt the moral high ground slipping away. "If the Document proves the true days of the crucifixion and resurrection, why keep it to yourself? Rock would've done the right thing with it. You didn't have to kill him." Scribe's cheeks tightened.

"Oh, but I did. You see, these people I mentioned know we have the Document. And the only thing that has kept the Coptic Church from genocide is our agreement to never allow it to surface in the outside world. Your friend obviously thought the world having access to the Document is worth the lives of our people. We disagree."

Rifling through his thoughts, Wahid interrogated Habash. "So *you* tampered with the phone records?"

Habash shifted his gaze. "I didn't tamper with the records. The call did come from Scribe's phone, which I retrieved when I secured his luggage on Wednesday. I was scheduled to pick him up at the airport as a favor to Delores. But all that arrived was his bag and... well, you know the rest."

Wahid followed the trail. "And you used Scribe's phone to lure Rockman to St. George's before murdering him and put it back before Mari picked up the bag on Friday."

Habash titled his head and shrugged his shoulders. "Inspector, murder is such an ugly word. I prefer to think of it as restorative justice in defense of our people upon a betrayer of a sacred trust."

"So Chief, you were going to let an innocent man, his friend, suffer for your crimes?"

Habash sighed and spoke emphatically. "Lamir, our people were chosen to protect Christ from the very beginning. God sent him to us when Herod sought his life and we protected him in this very place. When Magdalene and the child came to us we sheltered them here, where we now stand. It was only right that when St. Mark came here to establish the first church, he gave us the true accounting of Christ's passion and the original *Didascalia Apostolorum* for safe keeping. How many lives do you think *we* have sacrificed to do this?"

"All this time I thought you were a Muslim."

"It is permissible to disguise one's intentions to ensure the fulfillment of God's will."

Mari lashed out. "Your deranged piety makes my skin crawl!"

Wahid stepped in front of her as a shield. "Who threatened to wipe out our people?"

Habash glared at Mari but spoke to Wahid. "The same ones that stood by and watched the Jews get exterminated in Germany. They even encouraged some of it. With all their power and opulence, they could have ended it; instead they did nothing. They didn't care to. Rockman either did not understand that or did not care. Either way, he had to be eliminated."

Scribe noticed Wahid using his hotel inch-move and helped participate in the distraction. "But that doesn't explain why you killed Saba and Adeena."

"Saba was unfortunate. In all wars there are casualties. I was watching while you spoke to the priest at St. George's. I would have taken you then, but Saba observed me in a compromised position and I could not allow him to jeopardize my mission."

"And Adeena? Why did you have to kill her?" Mari surprised everyone by speaking. The hovering Keepers remained silent.

"Another casualty. I followed you from the Semiramis through the souk and to the Synagogue. Who do you think caused the cyclist to lose control of his moped?" He sneered, then restarted. "I finally had you cornered when the Rabbi's girlfriend wandered into my path. My sources told me he planned to sneak her out of Cairo disguised as a married Jewess and marry her when they escaped. I couldn't take the chance that she knew of the Document."

Fire burned in Mari's eyes. "So you killed her?"

"Yes I killed her and I would kill you all to protect my people. As I shall."

A coldness filled the room when Habash closed his mouth. Then Scribe and the other hostages watched as tears stained his ruddy cheeks. "All the times I had to give puppet commands to shoot my people down like dogs! The sacrifice of a few saved the lives of many. I live with all these deaths on my conscience, but would gladly do it again to protect the Holy Church of St. Mark."

Habash pulled a second dagger from his left sleeve and an unsheathing echoed around the circle. Each Keeper held a blade in both hands and prepared himself for an early morning massacre.

Habash stood at attention with his eyes skyward and both knives facing upward as he yielded: "Elder, on your word".

Cocoa braved the moment but Scribe felt her emotions by the way she gripped his hand. Neither he nor Rockman ever thought they'd die this young, especially not like this. Maybe Scribe had expected to be funeralized in a church, but not murdered in one. Even still, this was no ordinary church. It had guarded some of the greatest travelers of history and hidden secrets that most people stared at without ever knowing. The life Rockman spent searching ended just after the find. Now that Scribe had found what his friend wanted him to know, it made the end of his life a bit more bearable.

With the grace of an aging feline, a diminutive form glided from the Keeper formation and stood before Habash with his blades parallel. His words seemed to ride the wind.

"Noble Khalim, it is only by the will of God that this Church has endured in Egypt for these many centuries. Because of Christ, we have labored in love to protect our people and this sacred artifact from the hands of the unworthy. You have done well to retrieve it and restore it back to its ancestral home."

Habash bathed in the old man's words, standing straighter and taller, still gazing upward.

Elder continued. "But how could it be that the place where our Lord took refuge has now become a killing field?" Habash's grin shrank.

"Where his followers are butchered day by day?" Habash tilted his head ninety degrees downward.

"And now the bond of peace between Jew, Muslim, and Christian has been strained by such an act of malice. In this holy place? It is senseless."

Habash stared deeply into the eyes of his teacher. "Elder, few for the many. It is our way."

"Yes, my son. It is our way, for us. It is not what we impose on others. Matthew was one of us and accepted the consequences of our path. These others had nothing to do with his actions and are innocents."

Habash tried to control himself, but his temples bulged as he responded. "But they know the secret!"

The Elder softened. "They know the true timeline of the Resurrection. It is in the Bible. That is not the secret we protect. In showing his friends the verses, Matthew did not betray us. Matthew betrayed us by stealing what he agreed to protect. He betrayed us by treating one people's lives as less important than another's. My son, in this you have also betrayed us."

Habash was incredulous. "I…I sacrificed my life to serve. How dare you accuse me of betrayal?" He pivoted his daggers ever so slightly.

The old man did not flinch. "Yes, you have sacrificed much. But you have also taken innocent life. You had the text after locating Matthew. The killing beyond that point was done while walking another path. Our ways speak clearly about those who kill the innocent. 'The one who knowingly sheds innocent blood shall not live'." Elder placed his daggers back into his sleeves.

Habash's eyes flamed red hot. "Old man, you have turned the Council against me. I will…"

"Khalim!" Elder grabbed Habash's wrists and bent them upward, causing his knives to clang against the dark stone floor. "Be honorable in death as you have been for most of your life."

Without turning, Elder spoke evenly to the group. "Brother Scribe, according to our code you are one of us in honor and spirit. If your friends agree to conceal what they have seen this day, on your word, you are all free to go."

Scribe shook his head before the words came out. "You have my word." The others echoed their promises of silence.

A shadow, only seen by Habash, floated along the posterior wall behind Scribe and the others before retreating. Its owner waded away from the barricade, noiselessly ascended the double flight of stairs, and ran full speed until he arrived panting at the garden gate of Maimonides Synagogue.

Elder spoke again. "Brother Khalim, take solace knowing that you will be with our Lord on this resurrection day."

The placid expression on Wahid's face conveyed a gradual peace that he didn't quite understand at the time. The answers to unasked questions had been given to him and it would take time to adequately appreciate their gravity.

As Scribe helped Cocoa and Mari scale the barrier, the circle of Keepers closed tightly around Habash. They chanted a prayer, vowed to remember him and the work he had done, then granted Habash the same rest he had bestowed upon Rabbi Rockman three days earlier.

FORTY SEVEN

The Cairo Opera House possessed all the glory and grandeur that made it the premier cultural arts center in all of Africa. Scribe and Mari scurried to their seats at the climax of the preliminary remarks. Chamberlain had the entire row reserved and fortunately she saved two seats on the end for them.

"Same old Scribe", she chuckled and reached over Mari to pat his knee. "Here's your laptop. You left it in my suite last night."

Scribe leaned in and held the computer. "Thanks. Could you hand it to Jack and tell him to keep an eye on it for me?"

Cutting her eyes to Mari and then back to him, Chamberlain smiled and obliged.

Many ambassadors and distinguished guests were on hand for the Unity Concert and applause greeted the Governor of Cairo as he took the stage and extended the official welcome.

Much of his speech had the excitement of leftover spinach, thanking the usual list of ministers and dignitaries, until he mentioned a familiar name.

"And to Ms. Cocoa Santana, on behalf of the city of Cairo, I wish to extend my deepest apologies for the inconvenience you endured…". Scribe's heart pounded audibly. *I know Cocoa didn't tell the Governor about the Keepers!* Then his mind registered the rest of the signals his ears tried to relay.

"...the inconvenience you endured... in your *workplace*. You are the kind of student that demonstrates the success of our exchange program and for that we are forever in your debt."

Cocoa rose in an elegant silk gown complete with gloves and matching purse, waving to the crowd like Michelle Obama. She rolled her eyes at the offending co-worker and popped back into show mode in zero seconds flat. Cocoa shot Scribe a knowing wink and gave Jack her hand when she was ready to be reseated. Jack almost missed the gesture because he was so mesmorized that he resembled Pepe Lepew the first time he saw his true love.

Even Rick admitted that Cocoa had risen to the occasion. Swinging his hand wide for a soul shake with Terry he crooned, "Carpe diem, my brother. Carpe diem."

Feeling like a newly released prisoner from solitary confinement, Cocoa sopped up their ovation like a biscuit in a fresh bowl of gravy.

The Governor resumed. "Thank you all for coming. Have a wonderful evening and, please, enjoy the concert."

The Westerville Choir dazzled the crowd with moving renditions of The Star Spangled Banner, America the Beautiful, and ended with the Egyptian National Anthem. The crowd of VIP's and professionals cheered like Jimmy Hendrix and Axel Rose had concluded an epic guitar-solo battle before their very eyes. Needless to say, Chamberlain was pleased to receive congratulations from Westerville's Board of Supervisors and reaffirmation of her appointment as President. As an added bonus, she'd been authorized to conduct a search for a new Choir Director as soon as she returned from Cairo.

When the crowd began to disperse, Scribe brushed against

the back of Mari's hand. Neither of them looked at the other. Instead they stiffened and faced forward, trying to pretend nothing happened.

Out of the blue, Scribe whiffed a nostalgic scent and heard a familiar voice in his right ear. "Lena says it's alright and she wants you to be happy."

He turned to find Gloria standing in the aisle looking more radiant than the first time he saw her. Scribe squeezed her like a child who'd come home after spending a month at summer camp. He remembered Mari and awkwardly pulled away before making introductions.

"Nice to meet you, too", Gloria replied. The twinkle in her eyes sparkled brighter than ever. "David, is this the lady you dreamed about? On horseback?" She tilted her head toward Mari.

"I don't know. I haven't figured out what that means yet."

"You will, don't worry." She pressed her purse to her belly and smiled with pride. "I see you found out what happened to your friend."

Scribe dropped his smile. "How'd you know?"

"Because his wound has healed and he is no longer grieved." Gloria laughed, revealing a beautiful set of teeth behind her full lips.

"What's so funny?", Scribe queried.

"Matthew said you owe him for saving your life at the church."

Scribe pivoted to Mari and skipped his palms together. "So it *was* his voice. I knew it."

"He also says he'll take good care of Lena and Amy."

Scribe's pores opened. "Are they there?"

"David, the ones we love are always with us; helping and

encouraging us to accomplish the work we are here to do. They were there when I met you, but Matthew's voice was the most urgent."

One of the dignitaries acknowledged by the Governor saddled next to Gloria with white gloves and full regalia, waiting for her to finish. "David, allow me to introduce you to Cairo's new Chief of Police."

Scribe spoke first. "Chief Wahid. Good to see you again."

"Likewise Professor Scribe." Wahid tipped his hat. "Mari."

"Lamir", she returned.

Gloria smiled. "Well, I see you all know each other. In that case, I must be going. Mari, it was a pleasure to meet you. I am sure we will meet again."

Scribe thanked Gloria with his eyes and released her hand to Wahid, watching them blend into the bustling throng.

"Are you alright?" Mari rested her fingers near the bend of his elbow."

"Yes, just processing it all."

"Well, what do you think about Jesus now?", Mari ventured.

Exhaling and lifting his eyebrows, he squinted and replied, "I guess I'm still thinking. But I sure do have a lot more to think about now."

A flash of mischief reanimated him. "Hey, are you ready to have some fun on my last night in Cairo?"

"I am at your service. What would you like to do?"

His eyebrows drooped and his cheeks broadened. "Whoa, that's a big question. The night is still young. Surprise me."

"David, your first surprise is that you're going to take me out for shawarmas. After that, we'll see."

www.ingramcontent.com/pod-product-compliance
Lightning Source LLC
LaVergne TN
LVHW091039080826
845145LV00002B/554

* 9 7 8 0 9 8 2 7 4 3 2 0 1 *